A TENSE WAIT

Roger drew back
steady. Then he
the door with h
loud—startlingly loud—and the door
banged again.

He heard footsteps.

He drew back, heart in mouth. He hadn't the least idea what to expect, knew only that someone was in the lighted room beyond. He heard a key turn in the lock—but the door seemed a long time opening. It opened at last—toward him. It struck his foot. He drew his foot away quickly, as light flooded out.

Also by John Creasey:

THE EXECUTIONERS
A PRINCE FOR INSPECTOR WEST
STRIKE FOR DEATH
BATTLE FOR INSPECTOR WEST

JOHN CREASEY

A PUZZLE FOR INSPECTOR WEST

HODDER PAPERBACKS

Copyright © 1967 John Creasey
All rights reserved

First published 1967
Hodder Paperback edition 1970

Printed and bound for Hodder Paperbacks by
Hazell Watson & Viney Ltd, Aylesbury, Bucks

SBN 0 340 12974 3

This book is sold subject to the condition that it shall not, by way of trade or otherwise, be lent, re-sold, hired out or otherwise circulated without the publisher's prior consent in any form of binding or cover other than that in which this is published and without a similar condition including this condition being imposed on the subsequent purchaser

CONTENTS

1.	ARREST	7
2.	FRANCESCA	15
3.	NIGHT CALL	19
4.	THE EMPTY SAFE	24
5.	THE PHOTOGRAPH	30
6.	CLUE	36
7.	SEARCH FOR CIGARS	42
8.	CHASE	48
9.	MORE OF MALONEY	55
10.	THE HAT	62
11.	NEWS FROM AMERICA	66
12.	NEAR MISS	73
13.	SILENT KANE	79
14.	FAMILY FRIEND?	86
15.	THE SECOND "NEEDLE"	93
16.	THE FARMHOUSE	99
17.	TWO PRISONERS	106
18.	SMOKED OUT	113
19.	SOME ANSWERS	120
20.	SUDDEN ILLNESS	126
21.	FARMHOUSE FIND	132
22.	COLD HOSPITALITY	140
23.	SHORT, DARK MAN	147
24.	THE LOVERS	155
25.	TOP FLOOR	163
26.	THE DOCUMENTS	168

1
ARREST

Chief Superintendent Roger West of New Scotland Yard stepped into the large room, and Chief Inspector Peel followed him. They left the door open, Detective Officer Burnaby's big frame strategically blocking the threshold.

A pale-faced man looked up from his desk, which was slantwise across one corner. Behind his gray head, wine-red curtains hung in deep folds.

A middle-aged woman, quite beautiful, sat in a winged armchair in front of the blazing log fire; shivering. There were dark patches beneath her eyes and her cheeks were pale. Lipstick slashed the pallor, scarlet varnish tipped the nails of long, white fingers.

Roger West stepped to the desk.

The woman gasped: "No!" in a strangled voice.

"You are James Mortimer Liddel," West said.

The man's voice was deep and firm.

"Yes."

"It is my duty to charge you with the murder of Lancelot Hay," West went on. "I must warn you that anything you say may be used in evidence." He moved round the desk and rested his hand lightly on the older man's shoulder. "I have to ask you to come with me, Mr. Liddel."

Liddel made no move.

"It isn't true," cried the woman, "it isn't true!" She sprang to her feet. "I tell you it isn't true; you're wrong to arrest him! You must be mad!" Her eyes blazed, but she could hardly get the words out. "You mustn't take him away!"

"I'm sorry, Mrs. Liddel." West sounded as if he meant it.

"I won't let you take him!"

"Don't, Mary," Liddel said. "The Inspector is only doing his job. You're making it worse for all of us."

"How can you be so calm? Anyone would think it didn't matter, but they're going to try you for *murder*. You sit there as if you were going—" The woman broke off, with a stifled cry.

"I didn't kill Lancelot, and so the police cannot prove that I did," Liddel said. "Mary, I want a word with the Inspector before we leave."

"They mustn't take you!"

"Francesca will be here tonight," Liddel said; "she will help you, my dear."

His wife caught her breath, turned as if she were going, then swung round, pushed West aside, and clutched her husband's hands. She flung herself onto her knees beside him, and buried her face against his coat, sobs wracking her body. The wide, loose sleeves of a dark-blue dress billowed, as if in the wind, the skirt spread over the wine-red carpet, a wide circle serrated with narrow pleats. Liddel stared straight in front of him, not at West nor at anyone. He looked tired.

Peel blew his nose.

"Come away, Mrs Liddel," West said, and took her arm.

Crying bitterly, she let him help her up. He took her toward the door. Standing behind the bulky Burnaby was a young, scared girl dressed in a maid's cap and apron.

"Look after Mrs. Liddel," West said to her.

The maid led the woman away, as Burnaby stepped inside and closed the door, as if to shut out the sound of crying.

"We can talk at the police station," West told Liddel.

"Very well." Liddel stood up. He was a tall man with broad shoulders, his hair still thick and vital. He was handsome in an impressive way. "I wanted my wife out of the room, Inspector. All I wish to say here is that you have been very kind. No one could have handled a distasteful task with more consideration. You advised me to be alone, but my wife insisted on staying." He paused, looking away from Roger. "All her life she has refused to believe that anything can go wrong. All her life —"

He broke off abruptly.

"We shall help Mrs. Liddel in every way we can," Roger said.

"I'm sure you will." Liddel's lips curved in a faint, sad

smile. 'When one gets knowledge of the police only at second hand, it is very misleading."

He looked down at three photographs on his desk—of his wife, of a young woman, and of a young man. He picked up his wife's photograph.

"She took that herself—a self-portrait. And the others—" He broke off abruptly, and put the photograph down. "Shall we go?"

As they left the room, two more detectives, from the division that covered the Kensington area in which the Liddels lived, came up the stairs. West stayed with them, to search the room and the rest of the beautifully proportioned Regency house. Peel and Burnaby went out with Liddel, into the cold March night. The last sound they heard as they left was that of the woman, crying.

The house was large, and every room hinted at wealth employed by a cultivated taste. Liddel, besides his pension as a retired senior civil servant, had considerable private means. Roger West went into room after room, but it was little more than a formality, for the evidence against Liddel was already strong.

He made notes of places he would search more thoroughly, later.

On the half-landing was a door he hadn't yet opened. He went in, and switched on the light. This was a small apartment, which had been turned into a darkroom. Two cameras, slides, films, all the equipment to gladden an expert's heart, were here.

"Go and get one of the servants," he said to the man with him.

The maid who had gone off with Mrs. Liddel returned with the Yard man; she was timid, nervous.

"How is your mistress?" asked Roger.

'She—she's terribly upset, sir. I've sent for the doctor."

"That's right." So timidity did not conceal a lack of common sense. The girl had intelligent gray eyes, which were candid and clear. "Who uses this darkroom?"

"Oh, it's Madame's, sir; she's wonderful at photography, she does all her own developing and printing."

"Does anyone else use the room?"

"No, sir, not really. Miss Francesca used to, now and

then. Mr. Liddel —" She broke off, moistening her lips. "*He* isn't interested, except in the results, sir. He always says he can't take a snap without moving the camera."

Roger smiled.

"I see, thanks. All right, you look after Mrs. Liddel."

* * * *

Two hours later, Roger West walked along the nearly deserted corridors of Scotland Yard. He turned into his own small office, which overlooked the Thames Embankment, and switched on the light. It was cold. He went to his desk, set slantwise to get the window light, and sat down rather wearily. He lit a cigarette and stared at a manilla folder on the desk. It was marked "Liddel-Hay" and contained all the records of the investigation of the murder of Lancelot Hay, whose body had been exhumed ten days before, and found to contain enough arsenic to kill a dozen men. He flipped open the file, and the first document was a note, printed by hand in block capitals, and not signed. It read:

LANCELOT HAY WAS MURDERED.

There was a rubber-stamped date on it: February 13. That was the day on which it had been received at the Yard. Attached to it was the envelope, made of the same cream-laid paper as that of the note itself. The postmark was London, S.W.1. There were smears of gray powder on both; but on neither had the police found a trace of a fingerprint they could identify. Beneath it were several other identical anonymous letters; beneath those, reports of interviews with the doctor who had signed the death certificate, all the trifles that had indicated the possibility of poison. Finally, the police had obtained an exhumation order. Now—

A man who was greatly respected by everyone who knew him; who had been a permanent under-secretary at the Foreign Office until his recent retirement; a prominent worker in the Church; a man known to be kindly and humane and generous was waiting to go into the dock next morning. And a highly strung, almost neurotic woman was virtually alone in a great house, apparently desolate and near despair.

It wasn't only that West felt sorry for them both; there was something else, something he couldn't explain but that made him question whether the evidence, which he himself had uncovered, was indeed foolproof. Anyone to whom he confessed this intuitive doubt would scoff at him; there was no need to let anyone scoff, but he could not silence his thoughts.

He heard footsteps, familiar and heavy. He wasn't surprised when the door was thrust open, and Chief Superintendent Eddie Day put his head inside the room. Eddie had a prominent nose, slightly protruding teeth, and a backward-slanting forehead; and nature had been mean with his chin. He grinned.

"Up late, *H*andsome?" Because he often had difficulty with them, he usually emphasized his aspirates.

"I wouldn't call it late," Roger said.

"It's nearly eleven." Eddie insinuated himself into the room, as if he weren't sure of a welcome. "You seem to smell the right time to be burning the midnight oil."

"Do I?"

"Anyone would think you had a private line to Coppell's flat, and know when he's roaming around. He's just come in."

"I didn't know he was on the prowl," Roger said.

"Some people would believe you," sniffed Eddie. "You've got Liddel tied up all right, I see. I 'and—*h*and it to you, Roger, you did a good job on that. How did Liddel behave?"

"He didn't throw a fit of hysteria, if that's what you mean."

"Wouldn't expect him to, too much of a gentleman." Eddie sniffed again. "The news-hawks are clustering round tonight. They're not giving the Back Room Inspector any peace at all. Big show for them, the Liddel case." Eddie came a little farther into the room. "Got some powerful friends in Fleet Street, Liddel has."

"Supposing we jump that fence when we get to it?" Roger suggested.

"I'm only warning you," said Eddie. "I—I think Hardy's coming." He paused for a second, his head raised, then winked and went out quickly, closing the door without a sound.

Eddy had ears as sharp as his eyes. He was the C.I.D.'s expert on forgery, and on his pet subject, shrewd and occasionally brilliant. For years in one of the divisions, he was now back at the Yard. His ears hadn't betrayed him, for heavy, deliberate footsteps could now be distinctly heard.

The door opened, and Coppell, the Assistant Commissioner for Crime, came in, closed it, and stood looking down at Roger. He was a massive man, dressed that night in light brown. He had thin, black hair, very smooth and shiny. His complexion was sallow. His dark eyes had a gimlet quality.

"Good evening, sir," said Roger.

"Evening," grunted Coppell, moving to a chair. He sat down. "What are you worried about?"

"I like some jobs less than others," Roger said.

Coppell lit a cigarette. "I've known you long enough to know when you're not happy. Liddel?"

"Well, sir—"

"It's late, we're alone, you needn't be formal," Coppell said.

Roger smiled. "Thanks! The truth is, Mrs. Liddel was hysterical, and the whole business upset me."

"I don't believe it," said Coppell. "I've never known you to let sentiment get in your way."

"The case stands up to every test I can give it," Roger reported. "Hay was a nasty piece of work, and it's been proved conclusively that he was blackmailing his uncle, who had a love child nearly thirty years ago. We can't find out where the illegitimate son is—and Liddel says he doesn't know. The blackmailing had been going on for five years. Add to that, dislike between them and recent quarrels. Liddel refused to pay any more hush-money. Add the note we found from the nephew, telling Liddel that unless he paid up at once, documentary proof of what he's doing would be sent to the press—that made it urgent, from Liddel's point of view. Add that Liddel bought arsenic, several weeks ago, that he met Lancelot Hay in a country pub, and went there using an alias. Add that death came soon after that dinner. Add motive, and the fact that the opportunity was of Liddel's own making. To make it worse, Liddel first denied having met his nephew at the country pub, and put up a false alibi."

"And you *still* don't like it?"

"I don't see Liddel as a murderer, and that's a laugh in itself. Half the murderers I've helped to hang seemed incapable of committing any crime."

"Any other line you can follow?" asked Coppell.

"None I can see. We've simply no trace of the illegitimate son. Liddel has two children of his marriage. Anthony, aged twenty-seven, is a bit of a libertine, hasn't lived at home for years, was on amiable but not devoted terms with his family. As far as we can find out, he stood to gain nothing from the murder, hadn't seen his cousin Lancelot for two years. On the night of the crime, he swears, he was in his own flat.

"Then there's the daughter, Francesca." Roger frowned. "She's been in the United States for the past three months, and before that had her own flat—the Liddel parents lived alone. Francesca left New York by air, yesterday. There are no other close relatives. Lancelot hadn't any money, that couldn't be the motive: Liddel has the only known motive."

"It all seems to add up," said Coppell. "The Public Prosecutor tested all the evidence before the warrant was sworn, and he's confident. I should try to get the thing out of your system."

Roger didn't speak.

"Not nursing any idea you don't want to talk about yet, are you?" asked Coppell, suspiciously.

"The only thing that really gives an excuse for wondering—is the spate of anonymous letters. All carefully cleaned of fingerprints, and we haven't a clue as to who sent them. Yet it proves someone else thinks he knows where Liddel was on the night of the murder. It also means that someone else hates Liddel's guts."

"So what you really think is that Liddel might have been framed," Coppell said, heavily.

"It's the strongest possible reason for having doubts," Roger said. "But I haven't found indications of anyone who would hate Liddel enough for that, except the anonymous letters. The love child's a possibility, but we just can't find him." He stood up. "Anyhow, that's the job of the defense."

"Who's handling it?"

"Potter."

"Couldn't have a better solicitor," Coppell said. "I wonder who they'll brief for the trial."

* * * *

At half-past twelve, Roger West put his car into the garage at his house on Bell Street, Chelsea, and stood for a few minutes by the front gate. The stars were clear and the cold wind had a knife edge; but he stayed there. The house was in darkness; which meant that Janet, his wife, had gone to bed.

He walked quietly to the front door, let himself in, then closed the door quietly. He turned into the room on the right of the small, square hall, and switched on the light. This was a friendly, pleasant room, well furnished, showing signs of wear and tear. On the table by his armchair, which backed on to the window, were two cartoons. One showed a burglar in his, Roger's room, with Janet fast asleep. Another was of two youths in front of a magistrate, who was saying: "Why don't you ask your father?" "He's always working, sir." His elder son, Martin—called Scoop and sometimes Scoopy—was the artist. He picked them up, and his smile became more free.

Roger poured himself out a whisky-and-soda. It wasn't long before he had forgotten the drawings and was thinking about the Liddel case.

He was halfway through the drink when a car turned into the street. He didn't really notice that, until it stopped outside. A car door banged. A woman walked up the narrow path from the gate. He reached the front door before the bell rang, waited a moment, then opened it.

The light shone on a tall, well-dressed young woman.
"Are you Mr. West?" she inquired.
"Yes."
"I hope you will spare me a few minutes," the woman said. "My name is Liddel—Francesca Liddel."

2

FRANCESCA

Roger stood aside, saying: "Come in, Miss Liddel."
She was quite beautiful, and she seemed calm. She was dressed in a smooth-textured, honey-colored coat with huge sleeves and a big rolled collar, and wore a wide-brimmed hat of the same shade. A diamond flashed from her right hand; she carried one glove and wore the other.
Roger waited for her to pass, then glanced at the waiting car. A man at the wheel was smoking a cigarette, but Roger couldn't see the face. He closed the front door and led the way into the room he had just left.
"Do sit down. Will you have a drink?" He smiled.
She stood by the fireplace, looking at him, puzzled. She seemed not to hear the invitation or the question. Roger went across to the drinks cabinet.
"Whisky, sherry, gin—"
"Thank you, I won't." She moved her hands, and the diamond ring on her finger scintillated.
"What's so puzzling about me?" Roger asked.
"You *are* Superintendent West, of Scotland Yard, aren't you?"
"Yes."
"I saw a photograph of you, in New York, and—oh, I suppose it doesn't matter."
Roger smiled. "In which I appear about seventy! I know the one. What made you take the trouble to find out what I looked like?"
"I heard you were in charge of the case, and a friend obtained a photograph of you from one of the New York newspapers."

"I see. I wonder if you'll wait for me for two minutes? Sure you won't have a drink?"

"Thank you, no."

He went out, left the door ajar, and hurried upstairs. The door of his bedroom was open. Light from a street lamp shone on Janet, who lay sleeping in the middle of the double bed, her dark hair loose over the pillow. The bedclothes were drawn up to her neck. He sat on the side of the bed and lifted the telephone, dialed 999, and was answered almost at once.

"Information Room at Scotland Yard: can I help you?"

"This is Superintendent West. . . . A car is parked outside my house. I want it watched and followed, and the driver identified. Send someone who's been working with me on the Liddel case."

"Very good, sir."

Roger replaced the receiver, and Janet didn't stir. He went downstairs slowly, trying to decide why Francesca Liddel had really been so puzzled. He thought he had had a vivid picture of her in his mind, but when he had opened the door, that picture faded. There was vitality about her fine gray eyes, clearly marked eyebrows, striking features that outshone memory, he would have guessed anywhere that she was James Liddel's daughter.

"Well, what can I do for you?" he asked.

She gave an unexpected little laugh.

"I expected to be shown the door!"

"It being improper to visit a policeman in his private home? It's been done before. Do sit down."

She sat down in Janet's chair, and he opposite her. She had nice legs and ankles.

"My father didn't kill Lancelot," she said.

"I can only act on the evidence, Miss Liddel."

"The evidence must be wrong."

Roger said: "Mr. Gabriel Potter is one of the best solicitors in London, and I've no doubt he will do everything he can to prove it. The last thing we want is to convict an innocent man."

"Is it possible to postpone tomorrow's hearing? There is one at the police court, isn't there?"

"There is one certainly, but I'm afraid it isn't possible to postpone it without new evidence."

"When must you have that?"

"By eleven o'clock in the morning."

For the first time she looked away from him.

"There isn't time. Mr. West, I don't like to think what will happen to my mother if that hearing takes place in the morning. She is very sensitive to public opinion. Suicide is a real possibility."

"A doctor can give her a sedative, or a tranquilizer."

"I don't think she would take them."

Roger said: "Miss Liddel, there are some things I should say to you, and some I shouldn't. This is something I shouldn't. We took no action until the evidence was so unchallengeable that we had no alternative. I don't think that new evidence will be forthcoming, certainly not in time for tomorrow morning. The responsibility for Mrs. Liddel rests on the defense. I'm sorry."

"What would *you* feel, if she really killed herself?"

"That the whole affair was an even greater tragedy than it is at the moment," said Roger, slowly.

Francesca leaned forward, holding out her hands. She said intently: "I don't care to accept all that responsibility, Mr. West. Please, don't misunderstand me, I'm not suggesting that it would be your fault." A quick smile accompanied the disclaimer. "I've arranged for a nurse to be with her through the night. I would be happier if it were a police nurse."

"Can't you stay with her?"

"It wouldn't be wise."

"Why not?"

"We were not on the best of terms when I left England, and my presence makes her even more hysterical. Mr. West, I want to try to make sure that there isn't a further tragedy, I want to make sure that an absolutely reliable nurse is on duty with her, night and day. Can't you arrange that?"

"I'd have to be sure that there is a serious possibility that her life is threatened," Roger said slowly. "Then I could give her protection. That's what you mean, isn't it? You're not worried about suicide."

Francesca framed her answer carefully. "I believe her

life to be in danger, and that she is in a desperate frame of mind."

Roger leaned across to the extension telephone by his side and asked for Chief Inspector Evans, who he knew would be on duty.

"West here. Will you arrange for a nurse to go to Mrs. Liddel, at 11 Maybury Crescent, and replace the nurse now on duty there? Our nurse is to be on guard against an attack on Mrs. Liddel, and may find her suicidally inclined."

"I'll get someone over there right away."

"Thanks." Putting the receiver back, Roger dropped his lighted cigarette and, under cover of picking it up again, was able to look at Francesca Liddel without her knowing that he was doing so. She took out a handkerchief and dabbed at her eyes, and was still dabbing when he looked at her openly. She relaxed, sitting right back in the chair. Roger stood up, went to the drinks cabinet, poured out a whisky-and-soda, and carried it across to her. She smiled as she took it.

"Thank you." She sipped. "Thank you very much."

For the first time, he saw how tired she was. It wasn't surprising. Less than forty-eight hours earlier, she had been in New York. The flight itself was tiring, added to which she had been weighed down by anxiety, and walked into a scene of hysteria; and she had confessed that she was on bad terms with her mother, who might be in danger.

She finished the drink.

"I must go," she said, and stood up. "You've been very kind." She held out her hand.

"All I want is the truth," said Roger, thinking wryly how trite and sententious sincerity could sound. He led her out and opened the front door, and as they stepped onto the porch she turned to face him.

'Who do you think wants to kill your mother?" he asked. The question sounded almost casual.

The light was good enough to show him the alarm that sprang to her eyes. She didn't answer, but hurried away. The man at the wheel had seen them at the door, and was now getting out. A street lamp shone on long fair hair and a narrow face—that of a younger James Liddel. This was Anthony, the "libertine" son.

3
NIGHT CALL

It was nearly two o'clock.

Roger sat with a whisky-and-soda by his side, cigarette between his lips, and his right hand on the arm of his chair. He waited to snatch up the receiver the moment the telephone rang, and so avoid waking Janet. The stimulus of Francesca's visit began to fade. Unless he gave himself something to do, he would doze off. He stood up, to get a book — and the telephone rang.

He snatched up the receiver.

"West speaking."

The caller was Evans.

"Word's just come in about Francesca Liddel. She went straight to 11 Maybury Crescent. The driver was her brother, Anthony, and it was his car. They're still there, and the car's outside."

"Has our nurse put in an appearance yet?"

"She will be arriving at any moment. Burnaby's covering the couple, and a patrol car is standing by. Want to be kept in the picture?"

"Yes," said Roger. "I'll wait up for a bit."

"How you love keeping your nose to the grindstone!"

It could easily be that he was making a mountain out of a molehill, Roger knew. Francesca might simply be waiting for the arrival of the police nurse, before leaving Maybury Crescent. If she were on bad terms with her mother, there would be nothing noteworthy about her going to spend the night at Anthony's flat. He, Roger, would be far better off taking his rest in bed. There was a lot to do before James Liddel went up before the magistrate for the first hearing.

He yawned again, and then heard a creak outside.

He sat up, and stared at the door. But there was nothing stealthy about the movements — someone was coming downstairs.

He was by the door when Janet appeared. She looked pale, the pupils of her eyes were heavy with sleep, her dark hair with its gray flecks was tousled. She wore an old gray-blanket-type dressing gown, and her feet were bare.

"That's a good idea," said Roger, "catch a cold." He kissed her.

"Why on earth don't you come to bed?" Janet grumbled. "Some people believe in sleeping at two o'clock in the morning." Sleepiness, the shine of cream on her face, and her untidy hair didn't make her unattractive. "What's going on?"

"One or two unexpected things about the Liddel case."

"Who were you talking to, just now?"

"I thought you were asleep."

"I don't mean on the telephone. I mean the woman."

Roger chuckled. "One of the unexpected things about the Liddel case! My sweet, she's lovely. She sat in your chair and made herself at home." He kissed Janet again. "Now that you're nice and jealous, go back to bed."

"I can't sleep"

"I don't believe it."

Janet said shrewdly: "You've been worried about Liddel all the time, haven't you?"

"I'm probably just wasting my time."

"You'd waste it more comfortably upstairs. You can always get up again, even if you do go to bed."

"I think there'll be a call in the next half-hour, if it's coming," said Roger.

"All right," said Janet. "Tell me all about it."

She sat in the chair where Francesca had sat, and a sense of contentment fell upon Roger, lessening his disquiet. He liked few things better than talking to Janet. He forgot that he was tired.

Before he had finished, the telephone rang again.

"Just to report that the nurse is with Mrs. Liddel and the others have gone," said Evans. "They're at Anthony Liddel's flat, in Hillcourt Mews, and he's garaged the car. Shall I tell Burnaby he can come off duty?"

"No, not yet," said Roger. "Tell him I'm going along there."

"Now?"

"Yes."

"Better you than me," said Evans.

Janet stood up, and said: "You get worse and worse. Must you go out, when everything seems to be going well?"

"The sober truth is that I can't keep away from her," said Roger earnestly. "Francesca, I mean. The ripeness of her beauty attracts me as a flower attracts a bee."

"Now tell me why you really want to see her again so soon."

"She's tired, nervous, edgy, and more likely to talk freely now than in the morning, when she'll have had a good night's sleep. If she really suspects that her mother might be murdered, she knows a lot we don't know. You must confess that the psychology is good."

Janet sniffed.

"I wonder what psychology would tell you to do if she were fifty-three and had hairs sprouting from her chin."

Roger put his head on one side, and then quite suddenly pulled her toward him. She was still breathless when he went out.

* * * *

Roger stopped his car in Hillcourt Street, which was between Grosvenor Square and Park Lane. It was a short, wide thoroughfare, with tall gray houses on either side. Here and there a street lamp shone. There were no lights at any of the windows of the houses. He left the car at a corner, near Hillcourt Mews. This was a narrow cul-de-sac; the buildings, once stables for the horses and carriages of the people who had lived in the great houses nearby, had been converted into garages and flats. A single electric light glowed over the wide green doors of a garage, a window showed a light. The surface was cobbled, making it difficult to walk silently.

Roger reached the spot where the mews widened into a square and saw a man standing in one corner, partly concealed by the shadows.

"Burnaby?"

Burnaby's monstrous shadow moved before him.

"Yes, sir." He glided forward, with unexpected stealth. "It is Mr. West, isn't it?"

"Yes. All quiet?"

"They're still up." Burnaby pointed to the light, on the second floor. "Been here about an hour, now."

"No callers?"

"None."

"Seen any shadows at the window?"

"I can't say I have," said Burnaby.

"I'm going to have a word with them," said Roger. "Stay here."

"Right," Burnaby said, sinking back into obscurity.

The front door was approached by a flight of stone steps. Roger mounted them slowly, turning over in his mind what he would say to Francesca. If she had secret knowledge, she would be more likely to divulge it now than at any other time; that was his only excuse for calling. He reached the front door. The light glimmered on a Yale lock, a bell, and a letter box; there was no knocker.

He pressed the bell, and heard it ringing. He waited, expectantly, but there was no answer. He pressed again; there was still no answer. He drew back, and looked up at the lighted window, but there was no shadow against it. He saw Burnaby moving forward, and pressed the bell for the third time. There was still no response. Alarm touched him.

"Burnaby!"

Burnaby glided to the foot of the steps.

"There isn't another entrance to this place, is there?"

"Not that I know of, and it's my manor. Won't they answer?"

"They haven't, yet. They may be dog tired."

"But why leave the light on?" Burnaby asked, and Roger turned to look at him.

It was fatal.

As he turned back, the door burst open. The shadowy figure of a man, wearing a trilby hat, his face covered with a scarf, rushed at him with an arm raised, a weapon in it—a hammer. He smashed a blow at Roger, caught him on the shoulder and sent him reeling against the rail. Roger began to topple. Surprise, pain from the blow, and the sudden fear of crashing to the ground, drove everything else out of his mind. He groped for the handrail, brushed it with his fingers but couldn't get a grip. He was vaguely aware of shouting and scuffling, lurched sickeningly backward, and then got a hold. As he steadied himself, his wrist twisted and he nearly let go.

He heard a man running, and caught a glimpse of a dark figure near the entrance to the mews. Another dark figure, down on the cobbles, was moving slowly.

"Burnaby!"

Burnaby grunted, and struggled up. He stood swaying, hands at his face. Roger saw that he had been hit across the forehead, and there was blood on his cheeks and nose. The sound of footsteps faded. The assailant was safely away now, there was little chance of catching him.

Roger said: "Take it easy, then telephone the Yard and put out a call."

Burnaby muttered again.

Roger made his way painfully back to the house. There was no light in the hall, but a faint glimmer showed at the top of a flight of stairs; this was a maisonette, with two floors. The bottom floor was grayly dark, but he could pick out the shape of doors and a narrow passage alongside the stairs, as well as some oddments of furniture. He went along the passage, flinging open the door, and found an empty dining room and a large kitchen, spacious and bright with tiles and chromium. There was no back door. He went up the carpeted stairs, making little sound, but the thumping of his heart seemed loud. He could hear nothing else, no hint that anybody was in the maisonette.

Three doors led off a small landing; it was from one of the three that the light was coming. He opened the first door, groped for and found the electric switch. This was a large bedroom, obviously a man's. In a corner were golf clubs, the pictures were all sporting prints or photographs. There was a small writing table and a corner bookcase. A double bed was undisturbed.

The second unlit room was a bathroom.

He had been there for about two minutes when he opened the door of the lighted room.

Francesca Liddel sat in an armchair. Her hands were tied in front of her, her ankles were tied to the legs of the chair, revealing silk-clad knees. She had something in her mouth, which looked like a handkerchief. Her eyes were wide open, showing great terror.

He thought it eased when she recognized him, but she turned her gaze away, looking pointedly toward the corner of the large sitting room.

Anthony Liddel lay on the brown carpet, with his legs bent. He was on his back, with one arm across his chest, and his head was turned away from Roger. There was blood on his ear and dark stains on the carpet.

He was lying by the side of an open safe.

4

THE EMPTY SAFE

Roger went on one knee beside Anthony Liddel, and raised his head gently. The blond hair was matted with blood; it was impossible to tell whether the injury was serious, but it looked bad. His pulse was beating. Roger stood up and went across to the telephone. Burnaby might have sent for help by now, but Roger dialed the Yard, arranged for a doctor to come, and replaced the receiver.

He took out his knife, went to Francesca, and cut her free. She moved her legs, moaning incoherently. Her wrists were red and swollen, the string—rough parcel string—had been tied tightly.

Roger pulled gently at the cloth in her mouth; it was a handkerchief, damp with saliva. It must almost have choked her. He put the handkerchief on a table, went out, and came back with a glass of water from the bathroom, and a towel. She hadn't the strength in her wrists to hold the glass, but sipped the water gratefully.

He dabbed her lips with the towel.

Anthony Liddel stirred, for the first time.

Francesca croaked a word that Roger couldn't catch.

"He'll be all right," he said, and took her wrists and began to massage them gently. She winced with the pain of returning circulation, and both wrists began to glow a fiery red. When he stopped, her mouth was less stiff and she could speak more freely.

"I'll manage."

She made an effort to stand up, but fell back at once. Roger helped her to a couch, and she sat down, with her legs bent, and began to massage her ankles. Her face was pale from the pain. Roger went across to Liddel, whose eyelids were flickering, and then knelt in front of the safe.

It was a combination wall safe, built unusually near the floor; obviously the combination number had been used. Roger breathed on the bright steel of the handle and the circular surround, but there was no sign of fingerprints on the clouded surface.

Liddel groaned.

The desk, a small one with the drawers wide open, stood near the safe. Papers and small books lay in disorder in each drawer. A bottle of ink had been upset in one, and the green liquid spread over papers and wood; some of the ink had dripped onto the carpet. Nothing else in the room appeared to have been disturbed.

There was a shout from the hall.

"You there, West?"

"Yes, come up!"

Heavy footsteps sounded on the stairs, heralding a short, stocky man with thick-lensed glasses, wearing a dark suit and carrying a bright-yellow pigskin bag. His waistcoat was wrongly buttoned and his collar and tie awry. He was Dr. Maltby, one of the oldest and most experienced police surgeons attached to Scotland Yard.

His gaze raked the room, settled for a moment on the girl, then on Anthony Liddel. He went straight across to the injured man, whose eyes were flickering open, and who was trying to sit up. Another man came in, a Detective Sergeant from the Yard.

"Seen Burnaby?" asked Roger.

"He's been sent home, sir—nothing to worry about."

"Good. Have you got equipment with you?"

"It'll be up in a moment, sir."

"Go through this room and then the rest of the flat. You'll find our man's been careful with his fingerprints, but he may have made a mistake about something else. Be careful with that handkerchief." He pointed to the one he had taken from Francesca's mouth. "Take special pains with the safe and the desk, and put all the papers on one side. I want to have a look at them."

"Right, sir."

Other men were coming up the stairs. They appeared carrying fingerprint and general equipment with them; one man had a camera. Flashlight brightened the room as photographs were taken.

Dr. Maltby stood up from Liddel.

"Well?" asked Roger.

"Not too bad." Maltby kept his voice low. "He could stay here with a nurse."

"Get him to a nursing home and have one of our men stand by," Roger said. "It wouldn't do any harm if he thought he was in a bad way."

"Up to your tricks? If he thinks he's at death's door, he might talk."

"You don't have to tell him what door he's at."

Maltby shrugged, and turned away. He had cleansed Liddel's head and hair, and the victim was now lying near the desk, a cushion under his shoulders. Roger went to Francesca, who was sitting up, gently rubbing her ankles.

"Can you walk?" Roger asked.

"Where do you want to take me?"

"To another room."

She got up without assistance, and was able to walk ahead of him. No one was outside the room, but a policeman in uniform stood at the foot of the stairs. Roger led the way into the bedroom, and left the door ajar. The girl went slowly to the bed, and sat down heavily, adjusting a pillow for her back. She had straightened her hair, and looked more composed; there was no puffiness or white ridges at the corners of her mouth, but her wrists were still red. Her stockings had been laddered, and her ankles were swollen where the string had been.

"Now supposing you tell me everything," said Roger.

"It was such a shock. I was going to stay here for the night. Anthony opened the door, and I came in—and a man dropped a sack over my head and shoulders. Before I knew what was happening—"

"Where was this?" interrupted Roger.

"In the living room," she said. "Anthony opened the

door and groped for the light, but the sack was dropped over me before it went on. Then I heard Anthony fall, and cry out. I tried to get free, but before I could manage it, someone carried me to that chair, and tied my ankles. Then he turned on Anthony again."

"You still had the sack over your head?"

"Yes," she said.

"Where's the sack?" asked Roger.

"The man stuffed it into his pocket before he left," Francesca said quickly. "But I could hear while it was over me. He was threatening Anthony; he wanted the combination number of the safe."

"And got it."

"I wouldn't blame anyone for giving it!"

"No one's being blamed," said Roger. "And then?"

"The man took the sack off me. He had a scarf over his face, and a hat pulled over his forehead—I could only see his eyes. He tied my hands together, and then started to ask me questions—he wanted something which he hadn't found in the safe."

"What?"

"He just said: 'those papers' and seemed to think I knew what he was talking about."

"And didn't you?" asked Roger slowly.

Francesca said slowly: "No, I did not."

She licked her lips; that may have been just because her lips were dry. There was a slight color in her cheeks, and her eyes were a little too bright, as if she were feverish. The wallpaper was cream colored, and her dark hair showed up against it, wavy and attractive, not unlike Janet's. The room was comfortably furnished, and large.

"So he wanted some mysterious papers that he didn't find in the safe," Roger said. "Yet he emptied the safe. Do you know what was in it?"

"Of course I don't!"

"You've been out of the country for three months, so perhaps you don't."

"Do you have to be insulting?"

"I simply want to get at the truth—why you were attacked and who attacked you. And I have to assume that everyone is keeping something back. That they so frequently are is always a policeman's disadvantage. What did the man look like?"

"He was about your build."

"And his clothes?"

"He wore a dark overcoat and a trilby hat—a very old gray trilby, there were stains round the band." She paused. "He wore thin cotton gloves, dark blue. And black shoes. There was a hole in the heel of his right sock."

Roger smiled. "That's pretty observant!"

"I had plenty of time to study him," she said. "After he'd knocked Anthony out again, he opened the safe and took everything out, and then ran through all the drawers in the desk. I think he would have looked in other places—but then the front-door bell rang."

"It's lucky I came."

"Why did you come?"

"To try to find out why you told me only half the truth tonight."

She didn't make any comment.

There was a tap at the door, and Maltby looked in. "Liddel'll be all right, but I've sent him to a nursing home for the night," he said. "Any help wanted here?" Maltby was notoriously a ladies' man.

"Would you like a doctor?" Roger asked Francesca.

"I'm quite all right, thank you."

Maltby strolled across the room, took her left hand, and felt her pulse. He made no comment, but when he had finished, looked at her wrists and ankles.

"You ought to have a salve for those, or you'll be stiff and sore in the morning. I'll send something round."

"You're very kind."

"And then I suggest you go to bed, and have some hot coffee," advised Maltby. "Plenty of sugar. This has been a shock, even for a girl with nerves of steel." Without any further comment, he went out of the room, leaving the door ajar.

"Where has he sent Anthony?" Francesca demanded.

"I'll find out and let you know later," Roger promised.

He stood by the side of the bed, looking down at her. A wardrobe mirror showed both their reflections; her face pale, his, tanned and set. She met his gaze, but as he continued to stare without speaking, she found this more and more difficult, and eventually looked away.

He said: "Murder's been done. You say you don't believe your father did it, but the evidence is very strong against him. Now you come along, believe your mother is in danger, and get savagely attacked. You may not know who attacked you or what the assailant wanted, but you do know why you're frightened for your mother."

She didn't answer.

"Your brother could die," Roger added.

She started. "No! The doctor said—"

"He could die. And if the blow had been only a little harder, he'd be dead by now. In all probability you're not safe yourself. There are other salient points," Roger went on. "The bad blood between you and your mother, for one thing—why is that? What's the truth about your family, Miss Liddel? Who do you think might want to attack your mother?"

She sat tight-lipped.

"You don't have to answer," Roger said. "There's nothing I can do to make you. But if you keep silent and there is more murder, the blame will be partly yours. Remember that. And whatever your secret is, it might throw new light on your cousin's death, and make the difference between life and death for your father. Remember that, too."

She still didn't speak.

"It's bad policy to withhold material evidence," Roger went on. "It suggests that there might be collusion between you and the criminals. Ever thought of that?"

"It's nonsense!"

"It's not nonsense," Roger said. "Personally, I don't trust you. I wish I could. It's a bad thing not to be trusted by the police, Miss Liddel."

She turned her head away, toward the door, distraught, disheveled. The door opened wider, and there was a bright flash—of a camera flashlight. Francesca gasped; from the door, a man chuckled. Roger strode across the room, but by the time he reached the door, the man who had taken the photograph was halfway down the stairs. He didn't look round.

"Thanks, Handsome! Nice picture for the *Record* in the

morning. Handsome West and Lovely Suspect!" He reached the narrow hall, dodged the policeman who now stood outside, and disappeared.

5

THE PHOTOGRAPH

Roger roared: "Constable, stop that man!" His voice echoed down the stairs, and the constable's answering shout floated up; there was another scurry of footsteps. Roger turned back into the room, to see Francesca straining forward, one hand at her throat, the other stretched out.

"He mustn't publish that! I look terrible!"

"Why not? You've been attacked, you wouldn't be expected to look your best."

"Oh, please get it back!"

"I can't tell a newspaper what it can print and what it can't. The cameraman had no right here, but he'll probably get away with it. His only crime was trespassing."

She closed her eyes.

"Didn't he name the paper?"

"The *Record*."

"Can't you ask them not to print it?"

"That would be a strong reason for them splashing it all over the front page," said Roger. "Does it matter so much?"

She didn't answer. "It's—oh, I hate the thought of it." She was distraught.

"Who do you think will attack your mother, Miss Liddel?"

She didn't answer.

"I hope that when you do start talking, it won't be too late," Roger went on.

He went out and slammed the door, but it didn't close properly. He stood outside for a few seconds, hearing no sound. The policeman hadn't returned. He pushed the door a few inches, and peered in. Francesca was still sitting on the bed, staring straight ahead, as if at a ghost. There was a photograph on the table behind her, a replica of the one on James Liddel's desk. So her brother had kept a picture of her in his own room.

Roger left the door ajar, and went into the room where he had found the Liddels.

The men were finishing their search, and Chief Inspector Peel, tall, blond, and good-looking, one of the brightest of the Yard's younger men, straightened up from the desk.

"Anything?" asked Roger.

"Some odds and ends of paper, but I don't think they'll help much, sir. Only two clear sets of prints—probably Anthony Liddel's. There are a few smears made earlier, I'd say two or three days ago." Peel wouldn't guess about that. "There isn't much doubt that the assailant kept his gloves on all the time. The handkerchief belongs to Liddel—it has the monogram A L on it."

"Go through the place with a comb," Roger ordered. "I'll have a look at everything in the morning. And keep an eye on the girl."

"Will she be staying all night?"

"Probably. But wherever she is, I want her covered."

"I'll see to it," Peel promised.

Roger went downstairs, and found a nervous constable, who confessed that he'd been bamboozled into allowing the photographer to enter, and hadn't been able to catch him. There was little point in rubbing the mistake in. Roger told him to keep his eyes open for anyone else who tried the same thing without the necessary authority, then he went to his car.

His wrist was painful, where he had twisted it, but otherwise he felt fresh enough.

He drove to the nearest telephone kiosk, called the Yard, and learned that Anthony Liddel had been taken to the Fairley Nursing Home, near Kensington High Street; it was only ten minutes' drive away. He soon pulled up outside the house, one in a tall terrace; the front-hall light was on, but the door was closed.

A middle-aged woman opened the door to him.

"What is it you want?" She sounded testy.

"I know we're being a nuisance," Roger said, and showed his card. "I'd like to see Mr. Liddel."

"Oh, the *police*." She drew back and her manner changed. "I'd no idea. *Every*body seems to be calling tonight. This way, please." She scurried toward the stairs.

"How is he?" asked Roger.

"Oh, there's nothing serious." The woman led him up two flights of stairs, and opened a door.

Anthony Liddel was lying back in bed, heavily bandaged but conscious; and when he saw Roger, he grinned. The grin was likeable; in all he had to do with Liddel's son, Roger found him amiable if unhelpful.

"What, another?" Liddel mocked.

Roger said, "Thank you," and the woman withdrew. A police sergeant, wearing a white coat, sat in a corner of the room. Roger waved him to stay there, and asked, "Another what?"

"Visit from a copper," said Liddel. "Robert, policeman, bluebottle, flatfoot." His voice was husky. "I can smell you people. You especially. I expected you to turn up."

"Criminals get that habit," said Roger drily.

"Only I'm not a crook! I'm not at death's door, either, and no one can scare me into making reckless statements."

"Who tried to?"

"Your doctor friend. Care to tell me what happened? I don't mind admitting that I thought I was on the way to Kingdom Come. Who rescued me?"

"I did."

"Thank you," said Liddel, simply. "That puts me in your debt."

"You can easily cancel the debt. Tell me what you know that you haven't told me."

"Nothing."

"What did the thief come for?"

The grin spread over Liddel's pale cheeks.

"Aren't policemen wonderful? Most people know that a thief pays a call to get whatever he can lay his hands on."

"This one was after something special."

"Your guess," said Liddel politely.

"Your sister's statement."

"You can't take any notice of anything Frankie said tonight. She was shocked. The man handled her pretty roughly. Which reminds me, I'd like to ask for better police.

You arrest the wrong men for murders, and let thieves get away with violence."

"We can deal with murderers and thieves, the people who cause us trouble are those who know a lot and won't talk about it," Roger said caustically.

"I know you've made a fool of yourself by arresting my father, and that's *all* I know," Liddel said, more sharply. "I want you to get out and let me have some rest. I also want you to look after my sister."

"If she won't help herself, there isn't much I can do about it," Roger said, reasonably. "Mr. Liddel, have you any idea why she should be worried about having her picture in the newspapers?"

"Frankie's funny that way—she's always disliked having her picture taken. Like me to tell you about when she was a little girl?"

"There's a nice portrait of her at Maybury Crescent," Roger said lightly.

"My mother took that. Do I have to hire someone to *throw* you out?"

Roger laughed, went out, and sat at the wheel of his car for several minutes. It was glaringly obvious that both Liddel and his sister were trying to hide something; in all probability that something was connected with their cousin's murder. But would either of them shelter a murderer at the risk of their own father's life?

He drove back to Chelsea, oddly dissatisfied and uneasy. It was half-past four when he got into bed.

* * * *

Chief Inspector Peel left a man at the flat, and superintended the removal of all interesting papers to Scotland Yard. He had no idea what Roger hoped to find, but because Roger had doubts about the Liddel case, Peel shared them.

He took a turn up and down the street. His own car was parked at a corner, near the mews. He was halfway along, when he heard a cry, turned sharply, and saw the constable standing by the corner, waving to him. As he reached the man, he heard a car engine starting up.

"Now what?"

"She's going out!"

"Did our man try to stop her?"

"I heard them arguing. Then she came down and went to the garage."

"Keep your eye on the mews," Peel ordered, and ran back to his own car. He was at the wheel when the girl drove out; he didn't have to turn round so as to follow her. She was soon in Oxford Street, driving fast; too fast. It wasn't unusual for the traffic lights to be ignored in the small hours, and she kept her foot down as she flashed past each one. Peel watched his own speedometer; he was traveling at nearly sixty.

Francesca slowed at Oxford Circus and again at Haymarket. She went round Trafalgar Square into the Strand at a good pace. In Fleet Street, where the road narrowed, Peel saw her head appear at the window, and she called to a man who was walking along the pavement. There were only half a dozen people about, but lines of newspaper vans were already in the side streets.

She drove another fifty yards, and pulled to the side of the road, opposite the imposing building of the *Daily Record*.

Peel was close on her heels, and heard a man inside the building exclaim:

"Well, what a surprise!"

There was a pause—and then Francesca said sharply: "Did you take that photograph of me?"

"Sure. You couldn't make a bad photograph if you tried, Miss Liddel!"

By then, Peel was in the large hall. He recognized the short, stocky figure of Flash Manners, whose reputation as a press cameraman spread much farther than Fleet Street. He had a genial, ugly face, and was smiling up into Francesca's; he had to look up, because he was only five feet three. He had a shock of ginger hair and thousands of freckles, and managed to look like an ingenuous schoolboy. His deep voice came unexpectedly from a small, soft mouth.

"I want it back," said Francesca.

"But Miss Liddel! I risked being warned off by Handsome West to get that picture."

"I intend to have it back. If necessary, I shall see your editor."

"Well, he wouldn't refuse to say hallo," Manners said. "And he's the boss. Shall I call him?" There were several telephones on a nearby counter. "It won't take two ticks."

Peel edged round the hall, so that he could see the girl more clearly. Her pallor struck him most, emphasized by the feverish glitter in her eyes. Her hands were clenched, as if she were making a great effort to restrain herself.

"I intend to have—" she began, and then stopped abruptly, and caught her breath. Peel watched her closely, and so didn't see the astonishment on Manners' face, as Francesca's fury melted, and tears sprang to her eyes. They might have been because of the release from tension; or they might have come from the sudden collapse of her self-control.

She said: "Please, I must have it," and her voice was husky. "It can't mean so much to you. I'll pay for it—I'll gladly pay for it." She stretched out a trembling hand, and touched Manners'. "Anything you ask. Fifty pounds—a hundred. Only, please, let me have that photograph back."

There was no answer.

"Any sum you ask," said Francesca.

Manners took her arm.

"Listen, Miss Liddel, I might do what you want if it were up to me, but it isn't. The Boss has it, and the block's being made, he's going to run that picture in the morning. If I know the Boss, a hundred thousand pounds wouldn't stop him from using it. You can try, but I think you'll be wasting your time. Can I take you home?"

She swayed, with her eyes closed; if Manners hadn't held her tightly, she would have fallen. It was almost too much of a good thing. She seemed to be physically ill, and Manners put his other arm round her waist. She was a head taller than he; beauty and an amiable beast.

"It can't be that bad," Manners said.

Francesca opened her eyes, moistened her lips, and looked over his head.

"I must see the editor," she said. "Please take me to him."

"It won't help," Manners insisted.

"Please take me to him."

Manners shrugged, and looked at Peel, and then turned and led her into the office beyond the hall. Peel waited for half an hour before she returned. Seeing her, it was impossible to tell what had happened. She appeared cold and aloof, walking like an automaton. No one was with her. She stepped into her car and drove slowly back to the mews. Not until she was safely there did Peel relax.

He no longer had the slightest doubt that there was something the police didn't know about the Liddel case.

6

CLUE

"Eh?" grunted Roger.

"Darling," said Janet.

"Hm?" Roger kept his eyes tightly closed.

"Darling," repeated Janet, touching his shoulder.

"No," grunted Roger.

"It's nearly nine o'clock."

"Ugh," said Roger, and opened one eye. It was broad daylight, and Janet was standing by the side of the bed. His vision was blurred, but she looked good. "What's up?"

"Like some tea?"

"No!" He closed his eyes again.

"You see what I have to put up with," said Janet.

"Let me have a go at him," said a man's sardonic voice; the unmistakable voice of the Assistant Commissioner.

Roger opened both eyes, started up, and immediately shut them again. Coppell loomed behind Janet. He was dressed in morning clothes, his hair shining with pomade.

There was a tea tray on the bedside table.

Roger licked his lips and cautiously lifted an eyelid.

"Good morning, sir. What's the trouble?"

"I have a social engagement at Woking this morning and I have to confer with the Home Office this afternoon, so I shan't have a chance of a word with you later," Coppell said. "What happened last night?"

"All details, or just what struck me as odd?" asked Roger.

"I've had the general story," Coppell said.

Roger ran his fingers through his hair.

"Miss Liddel appears to be terrified of a picture appearing in the press, and certainly hugs some secret. Anthony Liddel shares the secret. I think he's probably fooled us all along; we thought he was just an amiable waster, but there's more in him than that. I don't know whether the theft at the flat had anything to do with Lancelot Hay's murder, but it certainly gives us more to work on."

"Still want James Liddel up on charge this morning?" Coppell demanded.

"I wouldn't miss having him in dock for a fortune. I'll have two men in the public gallery, watching for reactions, and Peel in the court, to keep his eyes on the crowd."

"No idea why the girl resented the photograph, have you?"

"No. Has it appeared?"

"No," said Coppell.

"No," said Janet, and opened the *Daily Record*, which was folded on the tea tray. "There's nothing in here, which means that she found a way of persuading the editor not to use it."

Coppell said: "Yes, I thought that would impress you, Handsome. The *Record* is a scandal sheet, and the one way to make sure of getting scandal published in it is usually to ask for it to be kept out. She managed to get her own way."

"Has she any pull with the owners?"

"You find out," Coppell said. "You've a free hand to concentrate on this new angle."

"That's fine," said Roger.

"Are you sure you won't have a cup of tea?" Janet asked the Assistant Commissioner.

* * * *

Roger was at his office soon after ten o'clock, and went through the papers for the Liddel charge. He didn't expect trouble from Liddel's solicitors, but had to prepare for the unexpected. He intended only to make a formal charge and ask for a remand in custody. Even Gabriel Potter, *the* lawyer in such affairs as this, would hardly have the nerve to ask for bail.

There was no time to look at the two boxes of papers and oddments which Peel had brought from Anthony Liddel's flat. At ten to eleven, Roger was at the West London police court. At five minutes past, after he had been in the dock for four minutes, Mr. James Liddel stepped down, remanded in custody for a week. There had been no sensation, no suspicious visitors, for Francesca's presence in the public gallery could hardly be called suspicious. She looked regal and aloof; older than she had the previous night. All sign of distress had gone, she was holding herself on a tight leash. When she left the court, she turned her head aside, but several photographers took pictures; she walked to her car—actually her brother's car—and drove off.

* * * *

In the documents brought from the flat in the mews there seemed to be nothing to explain the burglary; and nothing to help identify the assailant. After two hours, Roger pushed them away. It was a little after two-thirty, and he hadn't yet lunched. He went downstairs to the canteen, and was halfway through boiled beef and carrots when a constable came hurrying in, looked round, and made a beeline for him. It was seldom that a Yard man looked excited; this man did.

"What is it?" asked Roger.

"Message from Mr. Peel, sir—he wouldn't wait to speak to you. He just said: 'Get to 5, Nye Street, Putney Common, quick.' His very words, sir."

"Go and start my car." Roger gulped down a couple of mouthfuls, and a swig of beer, and hurried in the constable's wake.

He was at the wheel within five minutes, and drove fast, stopping only to ask a policeman for Nye Street. It was in Barnes, at the edge of the small tract of open land designated by Peel as Putney Common. There were a dozen large, gloomy houses standing in their own grounds, and approached by long, tree-lined drives. Most of the gardens were well cared for, but that of Number 5 was unkempt. Last year's grass had been neither mown nor scythed, trees and bushes had obviously flourished unpruned for two or three seasons, dark grass patches and dandelions clotted the gravel paths.

Peel wasn't in sight.

Roger drove slowly past the house, and stopped. There was no opposite number; on the other side of the road a grass stretch led toward the common and the trees that dotted it sparsely. In sight, but some distance away, were more big houses.

Roger walked toward the gate of Number 5. The gate, once painted light brown, was peeling badly. There were marks of tires on the gravel, recent marks. He saw no sign of footsteps. Peel's nonappearance worried him. Roger glanced frequently up and down, expecting to see Peel at the next second, but five minutes passed and he didn't show up.

Roger stepped inside the gate.

He could be seen from some windows of the house, but the overgrown shrubs and the low-hanging branches of oak and beech trees hid him from most of them. The house was of red brick, and at the far side there was a typically Victorian turret with a spire; there was an appearance of solidity.

Peel should be on the lookout.

Roger walked farther along, then stepped off the drive to the grass of the shrubbery. He could no longer see the house. A bramble straggled across his path; he didn't notice it, and it caught his ankle; he unwound it impatiently.

"Peel," he called.

There was no answer.

He reached a spot from which he could see the corner of the house, and the garage that stood a little way back. The garage was closed, and there was no car. The house looked deserted. No sound of traffic reached here; he might have been in the middle of a dense forest. All his disquiet blazed up; there was surely no need to worry about Peel, yet he was worried.

He approached the house, watching the windows. He saw no furtive movement.

He went to the front door. There was an old-fashioned bell pull, and the bell clanged loudly when he tugged it. The sound faded slowly, leaving an impression of greater silence. Roger waited for a couple of minutes, then walked briskly round the house, reached the back door and saw an open window.

The window was wide open at the bottom, and he could see that it had been forced; the wood was splintered at one point. He strained forward, looking into the room beyond. It was an empty wash-house.

He would have been happier with a man in support.

There was ample space to climb through; he did so, and stood in the dingy, disused room. It had an old-fashioned brick copper, and in one corner was a long poker, rusty and covered with dirt. He pulled his right-hand glove on and took the poker.

He was surprised at the tightness of his grip on it.

He crept to the open door. A loose board creaked under his foot and made him jump. It was no use telling himself that he was a fool to feel jumpy; he *was* jumpy.

An inner door stood ajar, leading to a wide hall; and he caught his breath for he could see the soles of a pair of men's shoes. One of them was turned at an odd angle.

Roger pushed through the door gently; it swung to behind him. He bent low, stepping swiftly, prepared for an assault. There was none. He saw Peel lying stretched on his back, and Peel's head was battered much as Anthony Liddel's had been. Close to him was a long-handled hammer.

* * * *

The local police surgeon was young and prosy.

"This is bad business, very bad business," he said. "I can't possibly reassure you—I only wish I could. Serious injuries, no doubt—considerable bleeding from the lungs. I couldn't pass any opinion until after the X-ray examination."

Peel was already in an ambulance, on the way to the nearest hospital. The doctor and two divisional detectives stood with Roger in a huge, empty room. The house was untenanted, and no one had lived in it for several months. It was hard to say why the local authorities hadn't taken it over, but inquiries about that could come later.

Roger had been through it, from top to bottom; he need have gone no farther than the front room. Footprints in the dust that lay upon the boards showed that a man and a woman had been here. On the floor, trodden out, were two cigarette ends, each tipped with lipstick, which meant that Francesca had probably smoked them. There was no clue to the identity of the man. A tradesman, passing in a van, said that the car had left the house just after three o'clock; twenty minutes before Roger had arrived. Peel must have been attacked a little while before that.

"Believe me, I've done everything I can, everything," said the doctor. "And you were in good time—very prompt."

"Yes. Thanks."

The local men and the doctor looked at Roger, frowning, puzzled. His face was bleak, reflecting something of the mood of hatred stirring in him. Peel was not only a good officer, he was also a good chap. He'd come in here full of enthusiasm and eagerness—and he might die.

There was no clue on the hammer, and little chance of finding anything apart from the blood that stained the head, and some light-colored hairs—Peel's.

Roger asked suddenly: "How many men can you get here at short notice, Inspector?"

"As many as you want." The divisional man spoke promptly, keeping to himself his view that it would all be a waste of time. "Just tell me what you want done, and—"

He broke off, as a uniformed constable appeared in the doorway, a man of bovine expression who walked with solid, stately tread, and held something gingerly in one great hand.

"What's that?" the Inspector asked.

"Thought you might like to see it, sir. Found it in the grass. Three-quarters-smoked cigar—very black kind of cigar —*chee*-root, I think. Been smoked this afternoon, all right, still a bit warm."

Roger said softly: "Now that's just what we've been looking for."

7

SEARCH FOR CIGARS

Roger put down the telephone in his office, and Eddie Day, sitting on a corner of the desk and swinging his leg, asked hoarsely:

"What's the report?"

"No change."

"He'll peg out," Eddie said, almost as if he relished the thought. "Peel's a goner, take it from me."

"Need you gloat?" Roger's voice was thin, hard.

"Now don't get me wrong, 'andsome," Eddie protested, "no one would be sorrier than me if Peel died. Shocking thing. I've just got a feeling, that's all."

"And I've got some work to do," Roger said.

Eddie shrugged and went off. There was quiet outside, until a tram clattered along the Embankment. There was no sound in the passage—the Yard seemed to be hemmed in by an unnatural silence. Roger went downstairs to the canteen. On the way, three men asked if he had any news of Peel. When he reached the canteen, which was half full, he found the same quietude; every policeman's mind was full of a grim determination to get the assailant. Police work should be impersonal and dispassionate; an affair of this kind put passion into it.

A man called out: "Any news?"

"No change," said Roger. He went to the bar and asked for a cup of tea. "Anyone here with time on his hands? I don't mean duty time."

"Plenty." That was the first speaker, and there were murmurs from the others. "What do you want?"

"I want to find out who smokes a thin, black cigar, called Ramonez," Roger said. "They're made by a Dutch firm." He took a packet from his pocket, about six inches by three. It had a picture on it, of a smiling man smoking a long cigar. "They're sold in tens and fifties—the tens are packed like this, the fifties in wooden boxes. Probably only one tobacconist in ten stocks them. We're working the wholesalers officially, but Ramonez cigars have been on the market for a long time, it's impossible to be sure which retailers have them. Some may have been in stock for years. We need to find out who's bought some recently—within the past few months, anyhow. We haven't the men to put onto this job without neglecting other work—but we want to get hold of those buyers quickly."

He passed the packet round.

"Any idea of the locality?" a man asked.

"None at all—they might not have been bought in London. That would be our bad luck. I'm sending samples out to other districts, you won't be on your own with the job."

"Good enough," a man said.

Roger finished his tea.

"I think the man who attacked Peel smokes them," he announced, and went out.

There was silence in the canteen, even after he had closed the door.

Back in his office, he telephoned the nursing home. Anthony Liddel had run a temperature, and was likely to stay there for two or three days. His sister had visited him after the court hearing, but had neither telephoned nor called since. She hadn't been to see her mother, and hadn't returned to the flat in the mews. Roger opened the file on Anthony Liddel and ran through the list of the contents of the flat; cigarettes of three different kinds were mentioned, but no cigars had been found.

Already, a call had gone out to all police stations in England, Wales, and Scotland, for news of Francesca. No report had come in. It was impossible to say whether she had left the house in Barnes voluntarily. Peel couldn't talk, wouldn't be able to talk for some time, even if he lived. The only certain thing was that Francesca had gone to meet the man who had attacked Peel. There was no report on how she had received the message—Peel might know, but no one else did.

Anthony Liddel's car was in the garage at the mews; no one knew how Francesca had traveled to Barnes.

It was a little after six when Roger left the office, and drove to Fleet Street. He wasn't recognized downstairs at the *Record* office, but the moment he stepped into the newsroom half a dozen men looked up and two called out to him. The huge office was noisy with clattering typewriters, telephones, men and women talking. There were a hundred people here, at some fifty desks, and there was hardly room to walk between them. The tape was ticking out, in one corner. In another, a ginger-haired man with freckles looked up at Roger, grinning.

Roger went across to him.

"Hallo, Flash."

"An honor, I'm sure." Flash Manners grinned.

"This isn't funny."

"Okay," said Manners. "Any news of Peel?"

"Touch and go."

"I didn't know him well but I liked Peel," said Manners. 'We're doing him proud. You're getting plenty of space, too, you're still the glamor boy of the Yard. What can I do for you?"

"How much did Francesca Liddel pay you to destroy that photograph you took last night?"

"Oh, no, that won't wash. Strictly on the line of duty, that's me. She fixed it with the Old Man."

"Did she say why she was so anxious it shouldn't be published?"

"No."

"Didn't she give you a hint?"

"No," said Manners. He stood up. "If I could help you, Handsome, I'd do it like a shot, but there's nothing I can do. Better try the Old Man."

The editor's office was on the next floor. Even a Yard man could not gain admittance easily. Roger went into a large anteroom, furnished luxuriously with great armchairs and settees, a teletype, a television set, walnut-paneled walls, bookcases and racks filled with current issues of the betterclass magazines. In this sanctum sat a middle-aged woman austerely dressed, with prim, gray hair twisted severely into a bun. She asked Mr. West to wait, disappeared into another room, and quickly returned, to escort him to the editor's secretary. The secretary's room was smaller but no less opulent.

He, himself, was tall and willowy—a surprisingly young man with delicate complexion, sleepy brown eyes and hair swept back from a center part.

"Mr. Cardew is in conference, Superintendent, but I have informed him that you are waiting. He assures me that he will see you the moment he can."

"Soon, I hope."

"I feel sure that it will only be a matter of minutes," purred the exquisite. "Is there anything I can do for you meanwhile?"

"No, thanks." Roger found a cigarette in his hand, a lighter flaming gently in front of him. "Thanks."

"Would you care for a drink?"

"No, thanks."

"Then do sit down."

The exquisite smiled, as if he were delighted, and returned to his large, polished desk. There were some papers on it, but nothing to tie up with the frenzied activity in the newsroom. Roger leaned back in a deep armchair and looked at the photographs that adorned the paneled walls. They were all good. Each director of the *Record* was there—and, above the secretary's head, a portrait of the present editor, Raymond Cardew. Cardew was a personality, one of the strong men of Fleet Street. Almost bald, he had a high, wide forehead, and a broad nose; there was a Mussolini heaviness about his mouth and chin. He was brilliant and he was ruthless—and he had listened to Francesca's plea.

Why?

And why had she been so worried about that photograph appearing?

A telephone rang, and the exquisite lifted the receiver.

"Yes, at once," he said, and replaced it. "Mr. Cardew will be happy to see you, Superintendent."

Cardew's office was long and narrow, with a plain brown carpet and dark paneled walls; the only relief of austerity was a bowl of roses on top of a filing cabinet at one side of the huge desk. Cardew stood up. Unlike Mussolini, he was a tall man, powerful, with hunched shoulders and long limbs. His right hand crushed Roger's.

"All right, Alec." He nodded to the exquisite, who went out. "Now, how can I help the police, Mr. West?" He had a deep voice, which grated a little. The portrait hadn't shown the curious light-grayness of his eyes. "Whatever we can do, we will."

Roger was perfunctory. "I'm sure. Did you see Miss Francesca Liddel last night?"

"Yes."

"Did she ask you not to publish a certain picture?"

Cardew smiled; it was only a movement of his lips, and didn't touch his eyes.

"Yes, she did. I felt sorry for her, and was glad that I could help her. I had already decided not to use that photograph, Mr. West."

Roger said, "Oh," as if he didn't believe it.

"It often happens that we have to reject some of the best work," Cardew went on. "In this case, Manners had trespassed, publication of that picture might well have annoyed the police, and we always like to cooperate." The smile still missed Cardew's eyes.

"Very considerate of you," Roger said. "Did Miss Liddel say why she was anxious not to have it published?"

"No. She was in great distress, and very tired, and I was glad that I was able to reassure her. A very attractive young woman." Cardew moved a box of cigarettes across the desk. "But I'm not being fair, Mr. West! This is a peculiar case. Liddel is a highly respected man, and the recent developments show that there may be much more in it than we yet know. So—" He shrugged. "I was obliging, and later Miss Liddel may show her gratitude with an exclusive story."

Roger said slowly: "I see. And all she wanted was the photo killed."

"That's all she asked for," said Cardew. "But I think she really wanted some information. Although she was very upset, she was also very alert."

"What do you think she was after?" asked Roger.

Cardew shrugged. "I really don't know. She wasn't in any hurry to leave when I'd promised not to use the picture, and she wondered if I had any information which hadn't been printed. I hadn't, of course."

Roger said heavily: "I see. If Miss Liddel comes again—"

"I'll tell you," promised Cardew.

* * * *

Roger went to a call box and spoke to the Yard. There was no news of Francesca.

He went home.

* * * *

That evening and all of the next day, tobacconists in London found a remarkable interest being taken in Ramonez cigars. Most of those retailers who stocked them sold to regular customers. By nightfall on the second day, a list of fifty-one regular smokers of the brand had been discovered, and more reports were coming in each hour. It would be several days before each smoker could be interviewed and his movements, on the afternoon that Francesca Liddel disappeared, checked.

There was no trace of her.

Three newspapers played up her disappearance, her photograph, with averted face, was splashed in them and two others—but the photograph that Manners had taken didn't appear. Cardew was keeping his promise; for Cardew, with a journalist's nose for news, scented a sensational case.

Peel hovered between life and death. There was no report of interest from the nurses on duty at Mrs. Liddel's house. No one visited the Hillcourt Mews flat. Anthony Liddel was still in the nursing home, but likely to be out next day.

At home, Roger was silent to a point of moroseness. With a wisdom born of love and experience, Janet went to a neighbor for a couple of hours. Their two sons were away, and Roger was alone when a car drew up outside.

He was sitting in his chair, with a whisky-and-soda by his side; exactly as he had been the night Francesca had called. He started to his feet when the car door slammed, stood watching the passage door as footsteps sounded on the gravel drive. It might be anyone; it almost certainly wasn't Francesca. He was surprised at the way his heart thumped.

The front-door bell rang.

He didn't go immediately, but finished his whisky and lit another cigarette. Before he reached the hall, the bell rang again; an impatient caller. He touched the door handle as the bell rang for the third time.

He opened the door.

A man wearing a wide-brimmed, light-colored hat, a coat that was flung open, and a tie that seemed colorful even in the shadowy light, stood there.

"Mr. West?" The two words told Roger that he was an American.

"Yes."

"I'm glad to meet you," the caller said. "I'm Al Maloney." He moved forward, right hand outstretched; Roger took it. His grip was fierce. He was handsome in a curiously attractive way, he moved easily, when he smiled his teeth showed white and glistening—but there was tension behind that smile. "They tell me you're the man who can help find Francesca Liddel, and I sure want to find her."

A car engine sounded along the street.

"You'd better come in," Roger said; and stood aside.

A sharp report, like a backfire, came from a car as it raced past. But it wasn't a backfire. Roger caught sight of the flash from the rear of the car, saw a man's face show for a split second, but only in outline. Then he heard the American cry out, and heard a thud. Something hit the wall, bringing down plaster.

Roger thrust Maloney to one side and raced toward the road.

8

CHASE

Bell Street was long and wide, with small houses standing in their own grounds on either side. Five lamps spread a soft yellow light. The car from which the shot had been fired was still moving fast toward the far end of the street and the Embankment. Roger saw the rear light as he pulled open the door of Maloney's car and scrambled in. Maloney shouted something. Roger didn't hear what it was, and didn't wait. The car was a Chrysler. He stabbed at the self-starter, and the engine turned at once; he let in the clutch. Maloney shouted again. Roger started off as the American reached the car and wrenched open the door. He climbed in, breathless.

The car in front turned left, toward the Embankment. Roger swung out to take the turn without losing speed. No other cars were coming along the road, but the red light still glowed. Roger felt the nearside wheels bump the pavement, and shaved past a lamp standard before the car settled on the smooth surface.

Maloney slammed the door.

There were several turnings to the left; if the driver in front knew the district well, he could easily get away. He didn't turn left but right, onto the wide, smooth surface of the Embankment. Ahead, lights spanning a bridge gleamed on the smooth Thames. Lights on buildings at the other side of the river also gleamed in the reflection. The Chrysler held the road beautifully. The red glow in front kept steady. Another car came toward them, and by its headlights Roger saw the leading car, long and rakish; a sports model.

He felt a sudden gush of wind.

"What—" he began.

Maloney was pushing the windscreen up; the wind was coming through that.

The leading car passed the first bridge, and seemed to be heading for the West End and the city.

"You're not forgetting that man's got a gun," Maloney said, quite calmly.

"I'm not forgetting."

"Take it easy," Maloney said.

He also had a gun in his right hand. Roger caught a glimpse of it as they passed beneath a lamp. He was nursing it, and watching the red light. They were gaining. Two or three other cars came toward them and hummed past; in the light of one, Roger saw a man against the rear window of the first car.

There was nearly a hundred yards between them.

"Can't you go any faster?" Maloney demanded.

The speedometer needle was quivering on the eighty mark.

Roger didn't answer.

A constable standing on the Embankment shouted something; the words were carried away by the rush of wind. It was cold. A piece of grit flew in at the window and caught Roger's eye. It stung, and his eye began to water. The red light seemed to waver—but he thought it was nearer.

Maloney said: "We'll get them."

Roger grunted—and then heard a sharp report in front, followed by a clanging sound. He hadn't seen the flash, but saw the second; the man who had fired at Maloney was shooting again. The second bullet struck the bonnet screen and bounced off; Roger didn't know whether it came inside or went out.

Maloney fired.

The roar of the shot seemed loud, the flash bright. Roger's eyes were watering badly. He kept his foot down and fought against the blinding tears; the piece of grit was like a red-hot needle against his eye. He heard another roar of shooting, another flash—and a quivering line of light seemed to come from the car ahead.

The leading car swung across the road, turning left. As it disappeared, Maloney fired again. Then the road was blank, ahead of them.

Roger gritted his teeth as he prepared to swing round the corner. He thought he heard a sound, as of screeching brakes. He took the turn as another car came along the road toward him. The driver pulled out wildly. Roger swung the nose of the Chrysler into the side turning—and then saw the car he had been chasing, drawn up across the road. It was only fifty yards along, and the Chrysler was going at seventy. He swung left. There wasn't room on the road to pass the stationary car.

It seemed to leap at him.

The nearside wheels hit the curb, the car lurched, fenders scraped along a coping. The Chrysler lurched again, Roger lost control, and they swung round, then quivered to a standstill.

Maloney shouted: "There they are!"

Roger couldn't see.

Maloney pushed at his door, but the handle jammed. He banged at the handle, then pushed again. The door opened so suddenly that he nearly fell. Roger sat with one hand at his eye, the needle pains still shooting from it, the vision of both eyes hopelessly blurred; there wasn't a thing he could do.

Maloney went racing off; Roger heard him, and heard the roar of two shots.

He climbed out, wiping his eyes. He could see light now, but couldn't pick out the running men. He heard no more shooting, and the sound of footsteps faded. He returned to the car as fresh footsteps sounded, this time from behind him. He wiped his eyes again, and could see a little more clearly. A uniformed policeman came rushing up, and there was another behind him, as well as several other people; they all seemed to be talking at once.

The constable drew up.

Roger said: "Along the road—be careful, they're armed." He added belatedly: "I'm Superintendent West."

The constable turned at once and ran toward the end of the road. Half a dozen people stopped near the two cars. The second policeman, who had heard the tail end of the orders, came up.

"Did you say Superintendent *West*, sir?"

"Yes. Hurry."

"Yes, sir!"

But hurrying would do no good. If Maloney hadn't caught up with his assailants, the police certainly wouldn't. Maloney might have caught a glimpse of them; might know who they were, and be able to describe them. Short of that, there was little hope of catching them.

Roger's eye felt better; tears had washed the grit out.

Another constable came up.

"Better get some help and move these cars," Roger said. "Do the Chrysler first. Be careful with the other, we want prints from it."

"Yes, sir."

Roger watched them moving the Chrysler, wondered if it would be wiser to leave the assailant's car where it was until his men had time to go over it. He decided to do that, stationed a man at the end of the street to make other drivers take a detour and then approached the rakish-looking model. It was an old Lancia; there weren't many about. He took out his handkerchief and opened the door, careful not to touch the handle. A small gathering of passersby were now watching him curiously. Half a dozen policemen were here already, but there was no sign of Maloney or the man who had gone in pursuit.

Who was Maloney?

Roger used his torch, and its beam shone on the dashboard pocket, glistened on the windscreen and the instrument panel, reached another dashboard pocket—and then it stopped. His hand was steady at first, then shook a little. That didn't last long.

The light shone on a familiar picture—which was on top of a box.

Still using his handkerchief, he pulled the box out and studied the picture more closely. It was of a smiling man, smoking a cigar; and printed in bright red were the words: Ramonez—Perfecto.

* * * *

Maloney came up beaming; that didn't mean that he was amused. He held his left arm in front of him, awkwardly. Roger was standing by the car, looking at the box of cigars.

"Found anything?" Maloney asked.

"Not much. Did they get away?"

"You bet they did—but I'll catch up with them." Maloney's voice was low-pitched and bitter. "Do we have to stay in this place all night?"

"Until my men come to check this car, I have to stay. You needn't. Tell me where you're staying, and—"

"I only arrived in London tonight, I didn't lose any time coming to see you. My bag's in the car."

"How did you get hold of a car so quickly?"

Maloney grinned.

"I've friends in London. They had it waiting at the airport."

It might be necessary to check on his "friends."

"Can I go wait at your place?" Maloney asked.

"Yes. And you'll find a doctor at Number 15."

"Who said anything about a doctor?" Maloney demanded.

A police patrol car drew up, and Roger sent Maloney off in it. The crowd had grown larger, but no one asked questions. Then a squad car arrived. Four men, with all the equipment needed to check over the car, tumbled out. There was a photographer, two fingerprint men, and a sergeant. Roger gave them brisk instructions—they were to test every part of the car for prints, and take everything found in it to the Yard. He wrapped the box of cigars in his handkerchief and gave it to the sergeant, and was then driven to Bell Street in the squad car by a silent policeman. As Roger climbed out, the policeman said:

"Any news of Mr. Peel, sir?"

"No good news, yet."

"Very sorry about that, sir."

"I'm sure you are. Take the car back, will you? And have that Chrysler taken to our garage and repaired."

The front door of his house was open. He saw shadowy figures against the curtains at the downstairs window. He heard Maloney speaking, and then Janet say:

"Of course it will hurt if you don't keep still."

She was standing behind Maloney, who was stripped to the waist; his shoulders were broad and bronzed, the muscles rippled. A wound, which didn't look deep or serious, was at the back of his shoulder. Janet had a bowl of red-tinged water on a table, towels, and antiseptics. She was using a sponge. Another woman, a neighbor, came bustling from the kitchen with a fresh bowl of water. She stopped at sight of Roger.

"Thank goodness *you're* all right, Mr. West."

Janet started and turned. "Roger!"

"No damage," Roger said, smiling more brightly than he felt. "Patch up the restless American." He walked in, and stood in front of Maloney, who kept his head up.

"Your wife's a hard case," Maloney said. There was a smile in his eyes.

"You have to be, dealing with the hard-bitten."

"Hear him talk," said Maloney. With his hat off, he showed corn-colored hair, rather wavy, a high forehead, and clear gray eyes; there was something in those eyes that suggested that he was used to looking into long distances. Roger had an impression of strength and of character; Maloney was a man one could easily like.

Maloney said: "Seriously, West, I'm mighty sorry I brought this to you."

"You brought most of it to yourself," Roger said. "Did you see them?"

"Not close enough to say what they looked like."

"Any idea why they don't like you?"

"I can imagine a thousand reasons," Maloney said, "and I wouldn't know which is the right one." There was an edge to his grin. "Can't you make a guess?"

"They didn't want you to talk to me," said Roger.

"Could be." Maloney shrugged one shoulder. "Do you keep Scotch?"

Roger poured him out a stiff whisky, and picked up the soda syphon.

"I'll take it straight," Maloney said. There was perspiration on his forehead, the arm wasn't as easy as he was pretending. "Thanks." He tossed the whisky down.

Janet drew back.

"You'll do now," she said. "I've put a plaster on it. You'll be stiff for a day or two, that's all."

"Better than being a stiff," Maloney remarked. He picked up his shirt; there was a patch of blood on it, and a small hole.

"I'll lend you one of Roger's shirts," Janet said, and hurried out. The neighbor went with her, and footsteps sounded on the stairs.

Maloney said: "I guess it'll have a long tail, but it'll be better than the bloodstained one, and you're about my size. You didn't get hurt, did you?"

"No." Roger offered cigarettes.

"Thanks. I'm very glad about that. I wouldn't have liked

to have a cop's death on my conscience." Maloney drew at the cigarette, then took it from his lips and held it cupped in his hand. "West, I'm asking you something, and I want the answer pretty bad. Do you think Francesca Liddel has been kidnaped?"

Roger said slowly : "It could be."

Maloney growled : "If they've hurt her, I'll tear them to pieces. You bet, I'll tear them apart!"

9

MORE OF MALONEY

Dressed again, with his fawn-colored coat draped over his shoulders so as to take pressure off the wound, Al Maloney sat in an armchair, leaning forward awkwardly. Janet and the neighbor were in the kitchen, Roger was in his own chair, opposite the American. Maloney's face was pale and his eyes were too bright; almost as if the excitement had brought on a touch of fever.

Roger said : "Now I hope you'll talk."

"That's my trouble, I'm always talking."

"I mean, talk sense."

Maloney grinned. "I'm beginning to feel I could like you."

"Why did you come from the United States?"

"To help find Francesca, and if you can think of a better reason, tell me."

"How did you know what had happened?"

"Didn't I tell you I had friends in London? I telephoned one, at the embassy, when Francesca left New York, and he called me when he heard she had disappeared."

He was not likely to lie about having a friend at the embassy.

"Why were you so anxious to find her?"

Maloney said : "I'm kind of fond of Francesca."

"In love with her?" Roger asked gently.

"If you want to put it that way, I can't stop you."

"Are you engaged to her?"

"I've known her a month. I guess you have to know Francesca more than four weeks if you want to talk about marriage. She knows the way I feel, if that's what you're asking."

"When did you last see her?"

"At Kennedy Airport, before she took her plane."

"Why didn't you come with her?"

Maloney replied : "I had some work to do, and considered it important." He laughed without amusement. "Then I had that message. It didn't take me long to go to New York and take the plane."

"Why did you come to see me?"

"I can read," Maloney said. "I can even read English newspapers. There were three or four that said you were the policeman looking after Francesca."

"Where did you get the address?"

"I called a newspaper office."

"Which one?"

"The *Record*." Except for the glitter in Maloney's eyes, he looked normal; and the catechism seemed to afford him mild amusement. "They were most accommodating, and they'd heard of you. You seem to have a big reputation on this side."

"I'm a policeman, doing my job."

"And the most important one you've ever done is to find Francesca," Maloney said. "Don't get me wrong, West, I mean to find that girl, and nothing will stop me."

"Plenty will stop you, if you carry loaded guns about London."

Maloney grimaced. "That? I always carry a gun."

"Not in London, without a licence."

"You can fix that for me—after tonight, I guess I need a gun. So do you. One of the things I don't understand is the way your police go around without toting one." Maloney sniffed. "It's asking for trouble."

"You may be allowed to keep yours," conceded Roger. "You've certainly used one before. You scored three hits—two fenders and the petrol tank. It's a pity they ditched the car, or they'd have run out of petrol, and we'd have caught up on them. It's on the way to the Yard now, and yours is being taken to a garage—I'll let you know which one."

"Thanks."

"You were telling me why you took a plane to England," Roger said.

"I've told you all I can about that," Maloney said. "I'd take a plane round the world three times if it were to help Francesca Liddel." He spoke quietly, soberly. "Will you tell me something as straight as you can?"

"Try me."

"Do you think Francesca is dead?" asked Maloney.

* * * *

Roger wasn't prepared to say that he thought Francesca had been murdered. The strongest argument against it, he told Maloney, was simple; if anyone had wanted to kill her, why hadn't she been left dead at the Barnes house? Taking her away suggested she had been wanted alive. He also argued that there was no evidence that she had been carried off against her will. The newspapers could say what they liked, Maloney could think what he liked, but for all anyone knew, she had gone willingly. He labored that point, and the glitter in Maloney's eyes became almost ugly. He wasn't so handsome as he had seemed; his face was too thin, and his long chin too bony.

Roger finished.

Maloney said harshly: "You're telling me that you think she's fooling around with the criminals?"

"It could be."

"Not on your life," Maloney said. "Not in this world. Cops!"

He sat back abruptly in his chair and banged his shoulder. He lost color; it must have hurt badly. From that moment on, he said little. Even when he accepted Janet's offer of the spare room for the night, he did so as if he didn't really know what he was saying. Janet insisted that he should go to bed at once, with aspirins and a final hot toddy. Roger left him, lying on his uninjured side, just after half-past ten.

The neighbor had left by then.

Roger dropped heavily into his armchair.

"Need you go out tonight?" Janet asked. She had washed her dark hair, and it looked fluffy and attractive; she was good to see as she sat on a pouf in front of him.

"I hope not—I'll call the Yard." Roger made no move to telephone. "I suppose it was reasonable for Francesca to fly back home. It *was* reasonable. But why did Maloney fly over?"

"From what you said about Francesca, she would be like a magnet to *some* men."

"But was the magnetic influence strong enough? Maloney is pretty strong-willed. He took that shooting without turning a hair, was as calm as a man could be during the chase. He was armed, which means that he was half-expecting trouble. He was shot at, trying to talk to me. Did someone want to prevent that, or—"

He broke off.

Janet said: "I know what you mean, darling, why not say it? Did they shoot at Maloney? Or did they shoot at you?"

* * * *

Roger couldn't be sure.

Janet felt sure, but that was partly emotional. Yet there was more to indicate that he had been the intended victim rather than Maloney. If Maloney had told the truth, he had come to England because he was passionately in love with Francesca. Would anyone shoot him for that?

He called the Yard.

"You'd better come over," said Evans, "there's a lot of stuff to be looked at."

"Right. Any news of Francesca Liddel?"

"No."

"Peel?"

"A rather better report," said Evans.

"Well, that's something."

Roger was more cheerful when he drove to the end of Bell Street, and pulled up alongside a constable.

"Telephone Division and tell them I'd like a special watch kept on my house, will you?" Roger asked. "And no one is to be admitted, except Mr. Lessing. Have someone watch who knows Mr. Lessing."

"Very good, sir," said the constable.

No one was in Roger's office. It was cold. He sat down and dialed a Kensington number, but there was no answer. He told the operator to keep on trying. Mark Lessing, friend of his and Janet's over the years, would gladly spend the night at Bell Street. With someone else there, Roger would be happier. He went along to the fingerprint office, a small one where two men were standing over a wide bench, which was dusted with gray powder. In a corner were dozens of articles, bottles, tins, hammers—a great variety of them, waiting for collection; they had been tested for fingerprints on one case or another, and were no longer wanted. On another bench stood several things waiting for tests.

One of the men, tall and spindly and wearing enormous horn-rimmed glasses, looked up.

"Just on that car job, Mr. West."

"Found anything?"

"Not so much. Some prints, but there was nothing on the steering wheel or the door handle. They wore gloves tonight, all right. Picked up a few on the dashboard, we've got photographs of them. I'm doing a box of matches now, got a spanner, a pipe, an A.A. handbook, and some insulating tape to finish. We won't be long."

"Send the reports in, will you?" Roger said as he went out. He turned away from his office, making for the Ballistics Department. Two men, one in shirt sleeves, were peering through an elaborate-looking microscope at a bullet that was fastened into a brass vise. One was Evans, who had the indefinable look of a Welshman but not a trace of a Welsh accent.

"They the bullets out of the Chrysler?" asked Roger.

"Yes." Evans moved from the instrument. "Smith & Wesson .32."

"So it was an English gun."

"And why not?" asked Evans.

"I can always hope. Can we trace the bullets?"

"Should be able to," Evans said. "We've been pairing them up with other bullets we've never identified, but no luck—we haven't any record of that same gun being used before." Evans, who was a general-utility man at the Yard, looked at the ballistics expert. "But he'll keep trying. Anything else?"

"Not yet."

Roger went along to the office, and was there for ten minutes before the final fingerprint reports were brought in. There was no record of any of the prints found on the car or the things in the car—they'd not been made by anyone with a record. Several of the prints coincided with those found on the box of Ramonez cigars.

"Were these all new, or several days old?" asked Roger.

"Some of both," said the fingerprint man.

"And those on the box?"

"New and old. I'd say the man who usually drives the car smokes those cigars. Will that help?" asked the fingerprint man.

"Sooner or later, yes. Get the prints enlarged and leave copies on my desk, will you? Then send them round to all divisions, as soon as you can. Follow that with all Home Counties and provincial police headquarters, with requests for them to copy and send to all branches. If we can find that chap, we'll be halfway there."

Evans came in.

"Halfway where?" he demanded.

"To the man who was at Barnes when Peel was attacked," said Roger. "That's as far as we want to get at the moment." He stifled a yawn. "Sorry. There's another job for you, Evans. Contact New York and find out if they can help us with information about a Texan or Arizonian named Maloney, Al Maloney. He carries a Colt .32, and is an expert with it. He left yesterday on a Pan Am 707 jet, and reached London this afternoon—or that's what he says. Five feet eleven, lean, corn-colored hair, bony chin, gray eyes, no other visible distinguishing marks. Better cable, and ask them to telephone if they can help."

"So that's why you thought it might be a foreign gun," Evans said. "I'll do that right away."

"Thanks."

It was a glum ride home. Roger didn't quite know why. He had more evidence—or clues to evidence—than he could reasonably have hoped for a few hours ago. The existence of someone with a grudge against at least one Liddel was proved. The new mystery, which might lead to proof that the arrested Liddel was being framed. His uncertainty and disquiet had been vindicated, and yet he was still glum.

The policeman on duty outside reported all well; there had been no callers. Janet was in bed, and drowsy. Roger joined her, the mood still on him; he was glad that she didn't want to talk. Their two sons, Martin and Richard, were both away, Martin on holiday, Richard on location for a television company; without them, the house was very quiet.

The only sane reason for Roger's gloom was Francesca's disappearance.

It was senseless to blame himself; by sending Peel after her, he'd done everything he could. Yet he counted it a failure.

He went to sleep thinking of Francesca, but didn't dream. He was awake soon after seven, not willingly, but by a clatter in the street; a milk truck seemed to have crashed.

Janet got out of bed, and peered out of the window.

"A wheel's come off," she said. "I thought it was a collision at least. It'll wake Maloney," she added. "I wonder if he likes morning tea." Maloney had made quite a hit.

"Orange juice or coffee, more likely," said Roger. He looked past Janet toward the main spare-room door, which was opposite the bedroom. He frowned. "See that?"

"What?"

"The door's not closed properly." Roger swung himself out of bed and hurried across the landing, hitching up his pajamas. He pushed the door wider open, and Janet exclaimed:

"He's gone!"

A pair of Roger's pajamas was on the bed, slippers by the side of it, but Maloney, clothes, Stetson, and all, were gone. On the dressing table was a short note, thanking Janet, explaining nothing.

10

THE HAT

Roger lit a cigarette.

"That's stopped you thinking about work for five minutes, anyhow," Janet said after they had recovered from the shock. "Darling—"

"Hm-hm?" Roger asked absently.

"Did that man shoot at you or Maloney last night?"

Roger put an arm about her shoulders and kissed her hair. "I may have been a magician to my sons at one time, but I don't really qualify for second sight."

"That means you think it was at you."

"I don't, because I can't think of a single reason why anyone should try to shoot me. But to be on the safe side, I'm going to have you watched today. I'll ask Mark to spend a bit of time here, now that he's back. The odds are that Maloney was the intended victim. What did you think of him?"

"He was all right, I suppose."

"Meaning?"

"I don't know. He was so sure of himself, perhaps a bit too sure. But I thought he meant what he said about Francesca Liddel."

There was nothing new on Roger's desk at the Yard. He went along to the fingerprint room, and found a new man on duty. He glanced round the walls, looking at the heap of discarded articles in one corner. On the side of the pile was an old trilby hat. It had a curly brim, as if it had been weathering the storms for years, and the once black band was stained in some places and bleached in others.

"Where did that come from?" he asked, picking it up.

"Brought in with the rest of the stuff, I think, sir."

"Stuff from where?"

"The car—the one you chased, sir."

"Oh, was it? Any idea who brought it in?"

"I can find out."

"I'll find out," said Roger. He took the hat with him to

the office, and put it on his desk. Looking at it, by some odd chain of reasoning, reminded him of Francesca. He called up the sergeant in charge of the squad car that had visited the crash scene in Chelsea.

"Yes, I picked up the hat—it was in the road near the Lancia. I had a look at it, and thought—"

"Sure it was near the Lancia?"

"Quite sure, sir."

"Thanks," said Roger. 'What about that Chrysler?"

"Nothing serious, it'll be ready by midday. Where shall we send it?"

"I'll tell you later," Roger said. He replaced the receiver and picked up the hat again. There wasn't a chance of finding fingerprints on it, and he turned it upside down. The inside was stained, as with sweat, and the thin leather headband was nearly black. He rang for a sergeant and told him to take it to the laboratory and have it checked carefully —especially, for hairs or traces of brilliantine. All the time, he thought of Francesca Liddel.

He found the report from Maybury Crescent. There was no change in Mrs. Liddel's condition. There was none in Peel's either. Fifteen minutes later, after Roger had looked through various reports on other cases, the sergeant came back with the hat and a small envelope.

"Hairs?" asked Roger sharply.

"Jet black, sir, and five of them. We've had 'em under the lenses. Youngish man, judging from the condition of the hair. We've scraped the leather band, and the stuff's being analyzed to see if we can find out what brilliantine he used. I don't think there's much chance of identifying the proprietary brand, most of those things have the same base."

"Well, it's worth trying," Roger said. The sergeant went out, and Roger lifted the telephone. He was soon speaking to the matron of the nursing home where Anthony Liddel was staying.

"Oh, Mr. Liddel left just after nine o'clock, sir." The matron was emphatic and sounded indignant. "He was most *rude.*"

"Was he fit to leave?"

"He'll be foolish if he overdoes *anything*, Mr. West."

"Yes. Did he have a letter or any message this morning?"

"Not to my knowledge, and I would certainly have known if he had."

"Thanks very much," said Roger. "You've been very helpful."

He put down the receiver, picked up the hat, and squinted at it. It was as dilapidated a specimen as he was likely to come across, a pride only to a tramp. He went out, carrying the hat, and whistling. Ten minutes later he pulled up in Hillcourt Mews. No one was about. He went to the front door of Liddel's flat, and rang the bell, keeping his finger on it for several seconds. Before he stopped, there was a movement inside; but the door wasn't opened immediately. The movements continued; he thought he heard a whisper of voices, and rang again.

Anthony Liddel opened the door.

"What the devil—oh, it's you." He had a bandage on, turban fashion, and his face was pale; but he hadn't lost the rakish look. "I might have known it. I don't want to talk to any more policemen, I'm sick of policemen."

"That probably runs in the family," Roger said.

"Meaning what?" Liddel's voice rose.

"Whatever you like to think I mean, but I was thinking of your father."

Liddel shrugged and stood aside. All the doors in the flat were closed, except one that was ajar. Liddel moved across to it and pushed it open. It was the dining room.

"Well, what do you want?" Liddel was abrupt.

"I thought I'd welcome you home," Roger said.

"You might spend five minutes looking for my sister."

"She might spare the time to call me," Roger said.

"Don't be a fool!"

"About what?"

"How can she call you? She's been kidnaped."

"So now you believe everything you read in the newspapers," Roger said. He twirled the battered trilby round on his forefinger, and Liddel was compelled to look at it. He stopped twirling it, and held it out. "Recognize this?"

"No."

"Look again."

Liddel frowned, and studied the hat.

"I've seldom seen worse," he said.

"You've seen it before."

"I'm half-inclined to believe I have, but it might have been on a tramp's head. I don't remember you wearing it." The sarcasm missed fire, Liddel seemed genuinely puzzled.

Roger took off his own hat and put on the old one. He turned round slowly, as a mannequin on show. When he was facing Liddel again, the man said slowly:

"I can't swear to it, but it's very much like the hat that my assailant wore. I only caught a glimpse of it."

"Probably the same one," Roger said.

"So—you've caught him!" Liddel gripped his arm. "Who is he? Have you found Frankie?" His voice was suddenly taut, the last word came out with difficulty. "Damn it, West! Have you found her?"

"No."

"If you've caught the man—"

"I've caught the hat, and that's a start," Roger said. "While I'm here, what about changing your mind, and telling me all you know? What documents did the owner of this hat come for?"

"Oh, *that* old story."

"Your sister's story."

"She saw you were a romantic, and gave you something to romance about."

Roger laughed. "You're a hard nut, but I'll crack you. Cigar?" He slipped a box of ten Ramonez from his pocket, opened it, and held it out. Five nearly black cigars poked out of one end, the grinning face of the man on the box was turned toward Liddel. Roger watched the other closely, and saw nothing that mattered; slight surprise, perhaps, but no sign of recognition, nothing to suggest that the picture or the cigars were familiar.

"I don't smoke cigars until the evening, and seldom then," Liddel said. "No, thanks. What are you getting at, West?"

"The truth, the whole truth, and nothing but the truth," Roger said easily. He put the cigars away and took out cigarettes. "Who's your visitor?"

Liddel started.

"Eh?"

"Who's here with you, trying to hide from me?"

"Oh, don't be a fool!" Liddel tried to sound indignant, and succeeded only in appearing peevish. "I arrived half an hour or so ago, and haven't seen a soul."

"I don't believe you."

Liddel said harshly: "One day you'll go too far."

"Maybe. Perhaps there are some things you don't know. Your cousin was murdered, your father is under arrest, your sister has put up a mysterious act and then run away—"

"She was kidnaped!"

"Or she was kidnaped, which isn't likely. You were attacked for the sake of papers which you try to pretend don't exist. Added up, that's a significant total, but there are other things." Liddel tried to look away, but Roger's eyes held his with a kind of magnetism. "The first thing isn't so important—I was shot at last night. I don't like being shot at. The second really matters. A friend of mine on the Force was attacked and may die. I'm not going to use kid gloves any more, Liddel. Who are you hiding in this flat?"

Liddel didn't answer.

Roger moved toward the door.

It opened, and Al Maloney came in, with an amiable grin and a wave of the hand.

"Looking for me?" he inquired.

11

NEWS FROM AMERICA

"So it's you." Roger looked at the American distastefully. "The next time you need first aid, my wife will probably dispense it with a poker."

"That so?"

"It ought to be so. What made you think that Liddel could help you find his sister more easily than I could?"

"That was just a guess," Maloney drawled.

"I doubt it."

"You'd doubt anything," Liddel interpolated.

"Does that surprise you? Why try to keep Maloney away from me? Why lie about him being here?"

"My visitors are my business."

"Not now," said Roger. "Your visitors and everything you do are police business. We have that way with suspects."

"What do you suspect me of?"

"Complicity in murder, and it spreads to your accomplices, whatever their nationality," Roger said. "Why come here, Maloney?"

"Just for a talk with Frankie's brother," Maloney said. "I came to the conclusion that you weren't so good. Maybe Tony and I can get results quicker than you, and that's why I'm in England—for results."

"Be careful you don't find yourself inside an English jail. I shall probably want to see you at Scotland Yard."

He turned on his heel, went out, and was at the front door before either of the others spoke. When he walked to his car he sensed that neither of them was happy about that last cryptic statement. He put the hat on the seat beside him, and began to whistle again. Back at the Yard, he called for the Inspector who was in charge of the quest for customers of Ramonez cigars, then telephoned to have the Chrysler taken to Liddel's flat.

The Inspector, big, burly, and florid-faced, was named Sweeney. He was not noted for his amiability but recognized as being a bulldog at any job. He had another accomplishment, namely an extremely neat handwriting. He now presented Roger with a long list of names and addresses beautifully transcribed; there were three pages in all.

"These all smoke Ramonez cigars," he said complacently as if he, personally, had arranged it.

"Any more to come?"

"Bound to be a few."

"We'll start on these," said Roger, scanning the list. Besides the names of the smokers there were the names of the tobacconists who supplied the cigars. "We'll try the tobacconists first."

"With what?"

"That hat." Roger pointed. "We want a customer who usually wears that hat."

Sweeney shrugged.

* * * *

The hat was recognized by the twenty-seventh tobacconist they visited. The shopkeeper did not know the name or address of his customer, but for two or three months a man had come in once a fortnight for fifty cigars. He always came on the same day: a Friday. Today was Thursday. He hadn't been last week, so he was due tomorrow.

Roger's whistling was gayer as he drove back to the Yard with Sweeney and a Detective Officer.

Evans greeted him at his office, looking more smug and satisfied than at any time since the beginning of the hunt.

"Now what?" asked Roger, sinking into his chair.

"Peel's out of danger," said Evans, and his thin face lit up. "He'll be receiving visitors tomorrow. I've told his wife. It'll be a long time before he's about again, but he's practically past the fear of a relapse."

"Wonderful! When can he talk?"

"Fairly soon—we've a man with him."

"Anything else?" asked Roger.

"Not much," said Evans, as if that were all the news anyone had a right to expect. "There's a cable from New York. Maloney left on that 707 all right. He's a rancher from Texas, and owns the Lord knows how many cows. He's also a bit of a playboy, spends a month or two each year in New York and Miami."

"Married?"

"No. Aged thirty-six."

"Relatives?"

"Orphan," answered Evans. "Those New York police know their job. He worked up from practically nothing—struck gold when he was in his late teens, and having a good head for business is now where he is. I asked them if they could tell me where he met Francesca Liddel."

"Could they?"

"No. But they were seen together quite a lot at the Waldorf-Astoria and a few other high spots in New York. That reminds me, sir, we've never inquired what Francesca Liddel was doing in America, have we?"

"No."

"Might try that line."

"I've been getting round to it. You have a shot, will you?"

"Suits me," said Evans. "Oh, I knew there was something else. Bill Sloan telephoned. He's cutting his holiday short. He doesn't say whether it's because he's run out of Swiss francs or because he's anxious to help in this job, but he'll be back tomorrow. Your friend Lessing telephoned, too. He said you'd find him at Bell Street, any time after six tonight."

Roger grinned. "Things are looking up." He told Evans about the cigar smoker and the hat, and Evans was almost excited.

"We'll get there soon," he said.

"We'll get there," Roger amended cautiously.

* * * *

It was nearly eight o'clock when he reached Bell Street. Someone in the front room was playing the piano; and that meant that Mark Lessing had been as good as his word. Few amateurs could play the piano as well as he. Roger let himself in. There was a light on in the kitchen, so Janet was there. He went along, and found her grilling some fillet steaks. She looked calm and satisfied, pushed him out, and said that supper would be ready in ten minutes. He smiled contentedly as he went upstairs, washed, and came down again, whistling softly. Mark Lessing was still playing, and Janet called out.

"Two minutes, tell Mark!"

Roger went into the front room. Lessing sat at the piano, long hair over his forehead, lean body slumped forward, playing as if he were in a trance. Roger let him finish a Liszt rhapsody, and then clapped his hands noisily.

Mark didn't turn round.

"Infidel," he said, in a deep voice. He tossed back a strand of hair, and strummed the keys again. "How are you?"

"Buoyant."

Mark looked round, smiling. He was a good-looking man, but his face had a touch of austerity; some called it arrogance. His rather sallow complexion was clear, his dark hair gray at the temples. As he stood up, he took out cigarettes.

"Not now, we're going to eat," said Roger. "I'm glad you've made it."

"Serious trouble?"

"There's always just the chance, when people come and see me here, that someone will get the bright idea that Janet's a better target than I," said Roger. "Can you make this your headquarters for a few days?"

"I'm installed."

"Thanks."

"It's getting cold!" called Janet.

It was almost impossible to forget the case; to forget that he was a policeman. After the meal they sat for half an hour over coffee in the small dining room, smoking, talking idly.

Mark collected china, and was also an amateur criminologist, with several slim books on criminology to his credit; good books, which were always to be found on the bookshelves of thoughtful detectives. He had a fund of stories and reminiscences, always something fresh; and he had recently lived on the Continent for several years, but come back to live in England. The quiet, effortless, atmosphere was restful, bringing balm to Roger's tautened nerves.

"Now we'll wash up," Mark said.

"You won't." Janet was emphatic. "Go and sit down, Roger needs to relax. He wants to talk to you, too."

They talked, Mark doing most of the listening. He made little comment, but next day or sometime soon he would probably see something in the tangle of events that Roger hadn't noticed. His keen mind was restless and probing; he would have made a first-rate policeman, and Roger began to realize how much he had missed him while he had lived abroad.

They had an early night; and there was no disturbance.

* * * *

Coppell was at his desk early next morning, dour and taciturn. He pushed cigarettes toward Roger, and leaned back.

"You've heard about the smoker and the hat?" Roger asked.

"Yes, indeed."

"The shop opens at eight o'clock—it's at Hampstead. Evans and a sergeant have been there since eight, and I'll be there myself about eleven—that's the usual time our man buys his smokes. Until then, we're almost in a state of suspended animation."

"What do you expect?" Coppell demanded.

"Miracles," said Roger. "I'm going to see James Liddel, and then on to see his wife. Evans should have a report on Francesca's visit to the States, but the mother and father may add something he can't find. Maloney's an interesting new element, don't you think?"

Coppell scowled.

"You could be setting too much store on this cigar smoker. When he knows you've picked up his hat and his cigars, he may be dubious about buying them from the same place."

It was surprising how often the A.C. managed to cast a gloom, Roger reflected. He had not succeeded in shaking it off when he reached Brixton. The gates of the prison seemed to clang with even more than their usual despondency behind him. Two grimly efficient warders led the way to a cell, where Liddel was reading a newspaper. He looked very tired.

"Good morning, Mr. West."

"Good morning, sir. I wonder if you will give me some information about your daughter's visit to the United States?"

"If it will help you," Liddel said.

Obviously, he had no idea that Francesca had disappeared. He had encouraged his daughter to visit America, where he had several friends who would give her hospitality. She was interested in interior decorating, worked at it as a hobby, and had been eager to study the fashions there; that was all. Roger left him and went to see Mrs. Liddel, who was still in bed and looked years older than when Roger had first seen her; she confirmed what her husband had said.

"Mr. West, he isn't guilty of this terrible crime. I beg you to believe me."

It was painful to see her distress, but there was nothing Roger could do. Still gloomy, he went to see Evans.

Evans's report, built on various inquiries and two long telephone conversations with the New York police, confirmed that Francesca had gone on a combined holiday and interior-decorating expedition. Roger finished his rounds by a quarter to eleven, and drove out to Hampstead; he was more determined than hopeful.

The Smoke Shop, where a Mr. White had identified the hat, was near the Underground Station. Roger parked his car around a corner, had a word with a policeman to make sure that no one got in his way if he wanted to drive off quickly, and walked toward the shop. A man was busy pasting up advertising signs on a nearby window; that was the sergeant on duty with Evans. Evans himself was behind the tobacconist's counter, serving as an assistant. White, a small, bald-headed man with a bright if strained smile, was stacking cigarettes on his shelves. Roger went in for a packet of twenty Players. Evans made no open sign that he recognized him, but gave an imperceptible shake of his head. Roger strolled out, and went across the road. He had little idea what to look for, except that it was a man about his own size. Half a dozen men who might measure up to that description went in and came out of the shop, each of them showing a packet of cigarettes. The sergeant finished his work at the window, and busied himself packing the signs away in his bag. He would start next door, if necessary.

Three customers went into the shop at once. Each came out unaccompanied.

Roger moved, so that he could see into the shop when

traffic did not get in the way. He would have stayed on the other side, but for the risk that the customer might recognize him if he came along, and walk past. The traffic was thick, and a nuisance; if he had to hurry, he might find himself held up.

White had assured them that the customer seldom came in after eleven-thirty; it was now ten minutes to twelve. Coppell's warning loomed in Roger's mind.

A man approached the shop, and turned in; he wore a new hat, a gray trilby. It had that touch of newness that made it noticeable to anyone particularly interested in headgear. Roger crossed the road in a gap in the traffic. He was nearly at the opposite pavement when he saw another man approaching—the tall, supple figure of Al Maloney. Maloney, unsmiling, appeared to be deliberately dawdling. He appeared, also, to be watching The Smoke Shop.

Roger kept on the curb.

He saw Evans, inside, stretch up to get something off a shelf above his head: a box of cigars.

The man with the new hat was standing with his back to Roger.

Evans had the cigars in his hand.

"These the brand you want sir? Ramonez?"

"That's right."

"I wonder if you would mind answering a question or two, sir," said Evans, whose voice always dropped to one of monotonous calm when he was excited. "I am a—"

The man with the new hat swung round and rushed toward the street.

12

NEAR MISS

Roger saw him clearly.

He had dark hair and a pale face, thin lips, big brown eyes, heavy eyebrows. His nose was long and pointed, like his chin. He swung round almost as soon as Evans began to speak, and moved swiftly, his right hand dropping to his pocket. Roger darted forward.

Maloney cried: "West!"

Only a few feet away, he took a couple of steps into Roger's path. The man with the new hat swung right—slap into the sergeant. Some sixth sense seemed to warn him that the man was a policeman, and he kicked. He caught the sergeant in the groin, recovered his balance and took to his heels.

Maloney dithered across Roger's path.

Roger handed him off, sent him staggering, and raced after his quarry. Evans was almost level with him. Passing pedestrians, about their business, stood and stared. The man who smoked Ramonez cigars swerved off the pavement and ran in front of a car. Brakes squealed. It looked as if he would be knocked down, but he dodged, dived in front of another car, and reached the opposite pavement. He ran on, in the same direction. Roger kept going on the opposite side of the road, looking across, seeing his man only a few yards ahead—but a mile away, for all the good that was. Yet there were policemen about who could stop him. Evans kept on bellowing: "Stop, thief!" Roger waited for the first break in the stream of traffic, and raced across the road. He avoided a bus by inches.

His quarry had taken a side turning, dodging two policemen who were hurrying toward him. None of the passersby interfered, but a woman screamed. The man was running fast along a wide street, with blocks of flats on either side and, farther along, houses that stood in a tall terrace. Roger pounded after him, now a long way in front of Evans. He saw that his quarry carried a gun; so that was why the woman had screamed, and why no one had interfered.

Someone else was running after Roger, and keeping fairly close. This was almost a repeat performance of the chase from the mews, except that it was now full daylight.

The man turned into the second block of flats. A name was painted over the front door: "Bingham Mansion." Roger reached the entrance—and a shot rang out. A bullet winged past him, and he heard it hit against the pavement on the other side of the road. He dodged to one side, but approached the front entrance quickly, keeping close to the wall. He heard a whining sound; a lift in motion. Leaning forward, he caught a glimpse of the dark-haired man by the lift, the gun pointing toward the door.

A man drew up behind Roger.

"I told you you ought to tote a gun."

Roger said : "Give me yours."

"Not in a thousand years!" Maloney peered round the entrance—and the man by the lift fired. Maloney drew back, then poked the gun round and pulled the trigger, shooting blind. There was a thud inside, as the bullet hit the wall. The whining stopped.

Roger snatched the gun out of Maloney's hand, and went forward. He saw the fugitive stepping into the lift, backward. He swayed to one side, but the man didn't shoot again. The lift doors closed and the lift began to rise. Roger raced up the stairs. He could hear the lift moving, and would know when it stopped; it seemed to be going slowly. It was a floor ahead of him when the noise ceased and the gates clanged open. He reached the landing in time to see his quarry disappearing into one of the flats; the door banged.

Someone else was running up the stairs : Maloney.

The flat was Number 17.

Roger reached it and knocked with his fist.

"Open up! Open in the name of the law!"

Maloney came up, panting.

"Save—your—breath," he gasped.

Roger drew back, pointed the gun at the lock, and fired; the first bullet bit into the lock, splintering wood; the second hit metal, and Roger kicked at the door. It opened a few inches. He heard the agitated voice of his quarry at the telephone. He motioned Maloney aside, stood back, gun in hand, and then crouched low. He whispered :

"Push the door open."

Maloney, standing at his full height and to one side, leaned across and pushed the door quickly. Roger went forward, crouching. He caught a glimpse of the hunted man, gun in his hand, telephone at his left ear. He heard the roar of a shot, but the bullet went over his head. He fired. His bullet smashed into the telephone, and it fell, shattered, to the ground. He couldn't check the man's rush, knew that one bullet could kill him. He heard a shout—

saw the man about to leap, as he flung himself forward, butting him in the stomach. His victim gasped, staggering backward, and Maloney shouted again and came rushing in.

Roger straightened up.

Maloney was struggling with the man, holding his gun hand above his head. It was over, bar shouting. Roger stretched up and wrenched the gun away. As he stood back, he said:

"Take it easy, Maloney."

They were wasted words. Maloney broke away, then hit the prisoner. The crack of the blow sounded loud, all Maloney's strength was behind it. The man with the black hair sagged, and his head jerked back. Maloney hit him again with the same savage strength, and he toppled over. Maloney went at him like a wild cat, clawing at his throat, getting his fingers round the slim neck. Roger could see only Maloney's profile; but his lips were twisted and his eyes were glaring, there was death in his hands and in his mind.

Roger hit him on the nape of the neck with the butt of the gun; hard. Maloney gasped, and his hold slackened. Roger pushed him away, as Evans and the sergeant came in.

"Got him?" cried Evans.

"It ought to help," Roger said.

* * * *

The prisoner's name, according to the papers he carried in his pocket and the information of the porter at the flats, was Kane—Louis Kane. He looked young, in the late twenties. He was still unconscious, and lying on the floor in the front room of the flat. Maloney, coming round, sprawled in a chair.

Kane's face had a vicious look, even when in forced repose. There was evil in his thin, pale lips. His clothes were cheap and threadbare, matching the old hat but not this flat, which must have cost six hundred pounds a year at least. Everything had been taken from his pockets and was now placed neatly on a long, narrow table that stood against one wall. Evans and the sergeant were already looking through the other rooms, the sound of their movements came clearly. A policeman stood on duty outside. The porter had been dismissed, and Roger was alone in this outer room, with the two unconscious men. There was no other telephone here, but he had sent a message to the Yard. Others would soon be arriving to start a detailed search of the flat. He didn't want to be out of the room when either Maloney or Kane came round.

Maloney opened his eyes first.

He blinked, licked his lips, caught sight of Roger and gave a grin; not much of a one, but it showed spirit.

"Howdy," he croaked.

Roger said: "You're under arrest."

Maloney struggled to sit up, but Kane didn't move.

"How come?" Maloney asked. "Didn't I save your life?"

"You nearly saved him from arrest."

"I don't know a thing about English law," said Maloney. "I'll have to get an attorney." He was so bright that Roger doubted whether he had been unconscious for as long as he had appeared to be.

"The charge is obstructing the police," Roger said. "And when we've got you in a cell, we can start questioning you. You won't be so clever afterwards."

"That's what I get for trying to help you," Maloney said. His grin had lost its spontaneity.

Evans appeared at a doorway.

"Can you spare a minute, sir?"

"If you stay in here, yes. What is it?"

"Go and have a look for yourself," said Evans. He stood aside, and Roger went into the next room. It was one of four others, a narrow, charming room, delightfully furnished; and the first glance told Roger that this was a woman's room. Another led off it. Roger went across, and looked into a woman's bedroom. On the dressing table, of figured walnut, was a photograph of James Liddel.

He picked it up. The photograph was signed: "For my beloved Francesca."

"See that?" asked the sergeant.

Roger nodded.

The flat belonged to a woman of taste; to Francesca Liddel. There were other photographs that he recognized;

probably more of Mrs. Liddel's work. Also, there were books with Francesca's name written on the flyleaf, several other indications, including clothes with her name on them, handkerchiefs with a monogram.

He went back to the front room, where Evans was now talking with two Yard men who had just arrived.

"See what I mean?" he asked Roger.

"I certainly do. No sign that she's been here lately, though."

"No," said Evans. "The man's been using another room, and living in the kitchen."

Roger nodded, and went downstairs. The porter told him that the flat was Francesca's, and that the man had her permission to use it. Did that mean she had recognized her attacker?

Roger took a closer look at Kane, and saw the marks where Maloney's fingers had raked his cheeks, and the red, puffy swelling at his throat; given another sixty seconds, Maloney would have killed the man. Had he deliberately tried to? Had he feigned that overwhelming surge of rage, but actually tried, coldly and callously, to squeeze the life out of Louis Kane?

If he had, it could only have been to prevent Kane from talking.

Roger felt Kane's pulse; it was beating.

Maloney said: "I didn't kill him."

"Not for want of trying," said Roger. "Take Mr. Maloney to Cannon Row, Evans. I'll see him as soon as I can get over there. Charge—obstructing the police in the course of their duty." He didn't look at Maloney, but waited for a protest.

There was none.

Maloney walked out, without assistance, but biting his lips as if he were in pain. He had used his injured shoulder much more than he should have done, and wasn't likely to be feeling comfortable. But in spite of it, there was a glint in his eyes, almost of satisfaction.

Kane was still unconscious.

"Better get a doctor," Roger said to one of the Yard men. "Have a police surgeon from the Division." He turned to the collection of oddments taken out of Kane's

pockets. There was nothing remarkable about
old wallet, of pigskin; good quality, but almo
There were keys, a lighter, two boxes of matches,
piercer, some loose change, a penknife, a small card
box containing a dozen cartridges for the Smith-Wesson.
There was a ten-size box of Ramonez cigars, with only
three left in it, a gunmetal watch, two combs, one with the
teeth missing, the stubs of two pencils, and a ball-type pen.
Except for the keys, nothing here was likely to prove
helpful.

Roger opened the wallet. A few stamps, three pound
notes, a registration card—Kane's—a driving licence, and
a photograph of Francesca Liddel made up the contents.

The photograph had been taken some years ago, but although Francesca looked younger in it, there was no mistaking her identity. It was creased at the corners, as if it had been carried in Kane's pockets for some time. There was no writing on the back; no notes on any of the papers, nothing to suggest where Francesca might be. She hadn't, it seemed, always avoided being photographed.

Unless there was something in the flat, or unless Kane talked, he was no nearer finding Francesca.

He went into the kitchen and looked round. Stacks of unwashed crockery were on the draining board, the tablecloth was stained and dirty. Kane had pigged it here alone, using fresh crockery as he had gone along. A fusty smell came from old tins, some of them coated with verdigris, which littered the floor beneath the sink. Tea-leaves overflowed a sink-tidy.

A man called out from the front room.

"Mr. West! He's coming round!"

13

SILENT KANE

The police surgeon, Maltby, was squatting on a corner of a table, looking at Kane, one eye half-closed, his ugly face set, and his lips pursed.

"Happened to be at the station," he said, as Roger went in.

Kane was licking his lips, and looking dazedly at the ceiling. He didn't seem to realize where he was or what had happened. He swallowed and gasped, then his right hand strayed to his neck, and he fingered it gingerly. He grunted again, and closed his eyes. Next time he opened them, the dazed expression had gone.

"Brandy?" asked Maltby.

"Just a spot," Roger said.

The doctor filled the cap of a brandy flask and held it to Kane's lips. Kane sipped and drank; swallowing obviously hurt him; talking would also hurt. He was now sitting in an easy chair, with a cushion behind his head.

Roger said: "The game's up, Kane, where's Miss Liddel?"

Kane looked at him, blankly.

"We know you're all right, and you can't hold out any longer. Where is she?"

Kane didn't speak.

"You're only wasting your own time and ours," Roger said, quietly. "Tell us where we can find her."

Kane drew in a deep breath.

"How should I know?"

"You know all right, you took her away."

"Forget it," said Kane. Talking obviously did hurt him, and his voice was a husky whisper. But the dazed look was gone completely; a cunning one replaced it.

Roger said: "You might find yourself in prison for life if you hold out on us."

Kane said: "That would be the day," and lapsed into silence. He refused to speak again; did not once open his mouth, at the flat, on the way to Cannon Row, the police station nearest the Yard, or when he was in the cell. Reluctantly, Maltby admitted that he was not fit to talk, because of the pain it caused him. But it wasn't the pain but his state of mind that kept him silent.

* * * *

Immediately after lunch Coppell came along to Roger's office and dropped onto an upright chair, which he overflowed; he never appeared to be comfortable except in his own capacious chair. He had a bovine look.

"So you were right about your hat."

"The luck broke my way."

"Has Kane talked?"

"No. I don't think he will."

"What have you found out about him?"

"Probably all there is to know," said Roger, picking up reports. "Ex-army, obviously a good education, family background not known, mixed with the wrong set, and started to live by his wits. The army gave him a few years of prosperity, but he was trained for nothing when he came out. He started several jobs, and was fired from them all. Lately, he's been on the fringe of one of the West End mobs, as a kind of contact man. He hasn't been inside, and we've never had tabs on him, but he's known to several of our men. They've marked him down as a possible bad man. The gun's an army relic, of course, and we don't know where he got his ammunition from, but that's fairly easy to come by. He's no family, no ties, and until three months ago, he was living in a doss house. He took over this flat a week after Francesca Liddel left for America."

"Do you know how he fixed that?"

"No—from the time he moved in, he's been a mystery," said Roger. "But Francesca knew him and must have recognized him as her assailant. I'd like to know why she said she didn't. He started to have money about the time he moved in—not much, but more than he's been used to. He had a hundred pounds in notes hidden under the mattress in his bedroom. We're trying to trace them, but they're all one pounds. According to the porter at the flat, he had no visitors—until this morning."

"Who went then?"

"Maloney."

"The porter sent Maloney up, and a cleaner in the passage heard a quarrel. Maloney was there about twenty minutes, and hung about outside afterwards. He followed Kane when Kane started out for his cigars. The things we can be sure about are pretty simple—Kane's being paid to do what he is doing. He doesn't care what he does. So, he was paid to go to Liddel's flat, paid to see Francesca Liddel at Barnes, paid to attack me—or Maloney. I don't think he has any other motive."

Coppell sniffed, and Roger smiled stiffly.

"We're part of the way. We now know that he was able to persuade Francesca to meet him at Barnes. We also know that either Anthony Liddel or Maloney knew where he lived—and the probability is that Anthony Liddel told Maloney. Which suggests that Kane may have some kind of hold over the younger Liddels. Remember, Lancelot Hay was a blackmailer; it could be that Kane learned something of it. Hay worked on James Liddel, Kane may have worked on the son and daughter. Something was strong enough to make Francesca let him use her flat, in her absence; strong enough to prevent them both from telling us about him. I'm pretty sure that they knew Kane attacked them at the flat—and still they wouldn't name him. So they're scared of what he might tell about them."

"And what could that be?" asked Coppell.

"Ought we to guess?"

"Yes."

Roger shrugged. "It could mean that Anthony knows the real truth about his cousin Lancelot's death. That Francesca knows something about it, at second hand. That Kane also knows, and is blackmailing them because he can give Anthony Liddel away as the real murderer. That would give a motive we haven't thought much about."

"Motive for what?"

"Lancelot Hay's murder. Because he was blackmailing his uncle, we've assumed that James Liddel was the only one with a motive. But if Anthony knew what was happening, Anthony might have killed Lancelot to save his father from persecution."

Coppell pursed his full lips.

"And the son who will make a sacrifice for his father lets the same father stand trial?"

"He will probably wait until the last moment, hoping that his father will get off. I warned you this was a guessing game."

"The sister?"

"She could have come back, been taken into her brother's confidence, and become party to it all."

"Not forgetting anything, are you?" Coppell was gruff.

"That Kane had a hold on Francesca three months ago,

or he couldn't have got her to let him use the flat," Roger said. "No, I haven't forgotten that."

"Not good enough," Coppell said. "None of it is."

"Guesswork never is," said Roger. "This all leaves out the wealthy Al Maloney. He could be all he's claimed to be. It's possible that Anthony Liddel took a chance, confided in him, or just told him that Kane was responsible for Francesca's disappearance. That could be enough to make Maloney go rushing to Hampstead. I don't know. I do know we'd have caught Kane earlier if Maloney hadn't interrupted. I also know that Maloney tried to kill Kane."

Coppell rumbled: "What's your opinion?"

"I'd rather back the first theory—that Kane is being employed by someone who still holds Francesca," Roger said.

"So now you've switched to the kidnaping theory."

"I'm inclined to. She could be hiding of her own free will, but I don't think that would serve any purpose for her. We had one piece of bad luck. Kane was trying to telephone someone. I've checked at the exchange—they hadn't answered his call, but there was a ring for Toll about that time and from that number. It suggests that he was going to telephone someone just outside the London automatic exchanges."

"Needle in the haystack again," Coppell said. "But the haystack's no bigger than the one you found Kane in." He hoisted himself to his feet, and was almost good-humored. "I hear Sloan's coming back."

"He'll be here this afternoon."

"Use him for this job," said Coppell. "By the way, Peel can see visitors, and by tomorrow morning he'll be able to talk. He might have overheard a lot of the conversation. See him yourself, won't you?"

"I will," said Roger, emphatically.

"Have you talked to Maloney yet?"

"I'm just going across to Cannon Row."

"Don't forget that Maloney's an American citizen, and if he thought he had a grievance, it would cause trouble."

Roger walked along the passages to the steps of the civil police building at the Yard, nearer Parliament Street. He stood on the steps, looking at the gray buildings, the gray paved Yard, the iron gates with the policemen on duty at either side. Cannon Row Police Station, squat and grim, was in a corner; it looked like part of Scotland Yard, was actually a divisional police station. He walked briskly across to it.

Maloney was in a comfortable cell. He had an armchair, a small table, books and magazines. He was sitting forward in the armchair, reading and smoking. The bars that fronted the cell were wide spaced, and he looked up as Roger and a sergeant, with the keys, appeared. He put his magazine down, but didn't get up as Roger entered. He looked pale, and his eyes were glassy; he'd obviously had a lot of pain from that shoulder.

"Say, West, you could let me have some American magazines."

"When Anthony Liddel told you about Kane, why didn't you tell me instead of going yourself, and threatening to cut his throat?"

Maloney said nothing.

"You went there straight from Liddel's flat. You were heard quarreling. You waited outside and followed him to the tobacconist's. You tried to stop me from arresting him. Later, you tried to squeeze the life out of him. You can't get away from facts."

Maloney's voice was gentle and drawling.

"I didn't try to stop you, I just got in your way. As I tried to get out of it, I wrenched my arm."

"The other things are facts you can't evade."

"You bet I can't, and you bet I don't want to. That heel manhandled Francesca. I guess I lost my head. But there was no harm done. You can't hang a man for losing his temper."

"You can jail him for causing grievous bodily harm."

"So that's your phrase," said Maloney. "Well, try it. I've decided to give you three more hours. After that, I shall ask for an attorney from the embassy—and you can bet your sweet life, I'll get one. If you want to make an international incident, hold me for three hours and one minute." His grin was broad, he looked as if he were enjoying himself.

"I can't think of a better way of making sure that I hold you," Roger said.

"I'll give a thousand dollars to any charity if you hold me here for three hours and one minute longer," Maloney said.

Roger shrugged, and turned to the door. The police sergeant jangled his keys. Roger went out, and the door clanged. Roger looked through the bars, and said:

"The Police Orphanage, and you can use my pen when you write the check."

He went off, leaving Maloney looking less sure of himself. But it hadn't really helped. Maloney hadn't admitted that Anthony Liddel had told him where to find Kane. He could guess as much as he liked, and still not be sure. It might be worthwhile seeing Anthony again, but he decided to leave it; a night of suspense might break down the man's resistance.

He made sure that inquiries were being made about Kane, then drove back to Brixton Jail.

James Liddel was playing patience, and he stood up as Roger entered, leaving the cards out on the table, placing the rest of the pack neatly on one corner.

"Two visits in so short a time, Mr. West?"

"Yes." Roger sat down and offered cigarettes. "Mr. Liddel, there are two questions I've never asked you before. They're important. I don't need to tell you that if the evidence weren't overwhelming, in our opinion, you wouldn't be here."

Liddel said: "That is right."

"The first question—if you persist in your plea of not guilty—"

"I most certainly do."

"Then whom are you shielding?"

Liddel smiled faintly. He seemed more rested than at the time of his arrest, and more imposing and handsome. It was easy to believe that he was taking all this philosophically, that the thought of death, now that he was used to it, did not worry him.

"No one, Mr. West."

"If you are shielding someone unknown, it might mean your death—and your shame."

"No one, Mr. West."

Roger said: "Very well. Do you know a man named Kane?"

"Kane—Kane? I recall it somewhere—but surely, Citizen Kane. It was the name of a man in a most remarkable film."

Roger said: "What about Maloney?"

Liddel started so violently that he knocked the playing cards off the corner of the table.

14

FAMILY FRIEND?

IN all their interviews the name of Maloney was the first thing that had upset Liddel's poise. He leaned forward to pick up the cards, in an attempt to cover his confusion. When he straightened up, all his color had gone, and his calm had gone with it. He moistened his lips, and looked away from Roger, placing the cards back on the corner with meticulous care.

Roger said slowly: "What do you know of Al Maloney?"

"I can tell you nothing that will assist you," Liddel said.

"I'm trying to save you from a serious charge."

"I thought your task was to get me convicted."

"My task is to get you justice."

"My lawyers will ensure that, Mr. West."

"They aren't likely to, if you keep information from them."

Liddel stood up, slowly. He had something of his daughter's grace of movement, and had recovered himself quickly; his voice was steadier.

"I would much prefer to have my legal adviser present at these discussions in future, Mr. West, and in any case, with or without him, there is nothing more I can say."

Roger turned to the door, touched the handle, hesitated, and then said slowly:

"It's a big thing to spend a life in prison for another person, Mr. Liddel."

Liddel made no reply.

Roger went to the governor's office, where the assistant governor, a youngish man, was alone at the desk. He was ready to talk, Roger anxious not to waste time. He used the telephone, dialing a Holborn number—that of Potter, Hughes, and Potter, Solicitors. He expected the office to be closed, but a woman answered him; and Mr. Gabriel Potter was in.

"I'd like to see him, in half an hour's time," Roger said.

"Just one moment, please." The woman went away, but the pause was only brief. "Yes, that will be quite all right, Mr. West."

"Thanks." Roger rang off, refused a drink, and drove straight to Lincoln's Inn. Here, in one of the dark-faced buildings that hid behind London's bustle, was a colony of lawyers—one of the thickest colonies in London. Everything was quiet. Roger went through an archway into one of the squares; it was like a university quadrangle or a cathedral close. There was a large square of grass, trim and neat; and flower borders, all well kept. He drew up at one side of the square, and walked round it, three times. It was cool and pleasant, and he wanted to have a clear mind when he met the redoubtable Gabriel Potter.

Potter's room was high, narrow, and long. The solicitor sat at an old-fashioned, leather-topped desk; and that anachronism, a quill pen, lay on a silver inkstand in front of him. There were hundreds of pigeonholes round the walls, each filled with bundles of papers tied in red tape; or with black deed boxes. Nearer Potter was a large safe, which stood much higher than the man himself when he was sitting down; and he was tall.

He was middle-aged, but prematurely white hair seemed to add more years than he possessed. His manner was mild, his voice soft and gentle. He had never been known to shout, never been known to give a harsh answer. His cheeks were pale pink, and his mouth was large and curved easily into a smile. Neither fat nor thin, he was dressed as his father and his father's father before him had been; and he sat in the same leather-seated armchair. His cravat was of dark gray, his waisted coat, almost a frock coat, lent him an added air of distinction.

Behind this exterior was one of the shrewdest lawyers in London.

"I'm very happy to see you, Mr. West," he greeted, standing up. "Please be seated. I wonder—as it is so late in the afternoon—if you would care to join me in a glass of sherry?"

"Good of you," Roger said. Potter was proud of his sherry.

He poured out, and handed Roger a filled glass.

"Your very good health and your continued success, Mr. West—with one exception!" He chuckled gently.

"I want to help to make it one."

"Indeed," said Potter with unruffled urbanity, but putting his glass down a shade too quickly.

"I don't know what Liddel has told you," Roger said. "It would probably be better if I did. I've just seen him. I asked him if he knew an American named Maloney, who is now in London. He made it obvious that he does, but refused to give me information about him."

"In*deed*." For all Roger knew, the name Maloney was as familiar to Potter as the name Liddel.

"I think the information he's withholding might affect the case," Roger said. "I also think that he is withholding it for personal reasons. I can't break down his resistance. You may be able to."

"I see," said Potter.

Roger said: "And it could be extremely important. I've spent a lot of time on this case, Mr. Potter. I've never been thoroughly happy about it—"

"How perceptive," murmured Potter.

"But the evidence is quite plain," said Roger. "There is one possibility which you may be considering. If you're not, I think it's time you started."

"So forthright," said Potter.

"It's a time for being forthright. The possibility is that Liddel's protecting someone else." He sipped his sherry and watched the solicitor carefully; and obtained precisely nothing from his appraisal.

"I have always been so convinced of the goodwill of the authorities," said Potter, "and this is a happy confirmation.

But if you have reason to suspect the existence of a different criminal, why not release my client?"

Roger said: "That was excellent sherry, Mr. Potter."

He had the satisfaction of seeing Potter's expression change, as he stood up, but it became again the mask of the shrewdest lawyer in London as he went with Roger to the door.

* * * *

A maid, the woman whom Roger had seen on the night when he had arrested Liddel, opened the door of 11 Maybury Crescent. The light was on behind her, and she recognized Roger at once, and stood aside.

"Good evening, sir."

"How is Mrs. Liddel tonight?"

"Oh, she is much improved," said the maid eagerly. "She's actually in the drawing room, sir, the first time she has been downstairs since — since it happened." The maid looked happier. "She's there now, with the nurse, and I'm sure she will see you."

"Tell her I won't keep her many minutes," Roger said.

The maid disappeared, leaving him in the hall. He remembered every detail of it. The atmosphere of prosperity and of culture was very marked. The Liddels had everything that money and breeding, education and society, could give them. There was a hush, everywhere; and it was broken only gently when the door through which the maid had gone opened again. She closed it as she came across the hall.

"Mrs. Liddel will see you, sir."

"Thanks." Roger followed her. The absurd formality of opening and closing the door, the opening of it again to announce him, seemed exactly right here. The years could pass and manners change, but with the Liddels, as with Potter, much remained unaltered.

The drawing room was large, with two chandeliers; a Bechstein grand; wine-red and dove-gray furnishings, concealed wall light, and other lights over the watercolors, a Russell-Flint and a Wimperis. Mrs. Liddel and the nurse were sitting near the fireplace; a log fire burned.

Roger was surprised; astonished.

Mrs. Liddel was as calm and composed as her husband. Beautifully made-up, she was hardly the same woman as he had seen on the night of the arrest, or on his last visit. The despair had gone, there was a kind of serenity in her eyes. Could it be due to rest or to medicines? Could anything like that explain the incredible change?

This was the woman who had been hysterical; whom Francesca had feared would kill herself.

She did not stand up, and did not offer her hand, but she smiled.

"Good evening, Mr. West. Please sit down."

"Thank you."

"You have no objection to my nurse being present, I trust?"

"None at all."

Cards were obviously a regular part of the Liddels' life. Mrs. Liddel and the nurse had been playing piquet; the board was on a card table between them, with the small pegs upstanding. By their side was another table, on which were a decanter and two glasses. He had not thought it likely that Mrs. Liddel would unbend sufficiently to drink sherry with her nurse.

The nurse, James, was a youngish, educated woman; one of the best women officers on the staff of the Yard.

"I hope you bring me good news," said Mrs. Liddel, in the same old-worldly way as her husband — and as Gabriel Potter.

"I wanted to ask you one or two questions which may help Mr. Liddel," Roger said quietly. He hesitated over the first, "shielding" question; and dropped it. "Have you ever met a man named Kane — Louis Kane?"

She said: "Not that I recall, Mr. West."

"He's a young man, with very dark hair, rather thin features." Roger took out a photograph and held it out. "Not a man you could easily forget, although he might have used a different name."

She studied the photograph, and handed it back.

"I have never seen him."

"Thank you. Have you ever heard of a man named Maloney? An American?"

The transformation was as remarkable here as with her

husband. The serenity was stripped from her eyes, something like terror replaced it.

Terror? Or hatred?

* * * *

Mrs. Liddel gripped the arms of her chair tightly, and closed her eyes, as if she knew that they were betraying secrets. The nurse stood up, and went to her, resting a hand gently on her shoulder. They were all silent, for what seemed a long time; only the gentle crackling of the burning logs broke the silence.

"A long time ago, Mr. West, I knew a Mr. Maloney. He was a family friend." She paused. "Why do you ask?"

"Have you seen or heard from him lately?"

"No."

"How long ago was it, Mrs. Liddel?"

"Many years ago. He went to live in America."

"How old would he be today?"

"How old?" She had recovered her composure completely, now. "It's hard to say. Fifty-five perhaps, about that, I should think."

That meant that the younger Al Maloney might be the son of the man she had known.

Mrs. Liddel told him nothing more.

* * * *

Roger waited at the Yard for half an hour before telephoning the Maybury Crescent house and asking for Nurse James. He had to hold on for several minutes, and the nurse sounded breathless when at last she spoke.

"Yes, who is it?"

"Superintendent West."

"I was hoping you would call, sir." Nurse James's voice was portentous, but subdued. "Mrs. Liddel collapsed after you'd gone, and I had to send for the doctor. She is in bed again, and quite prostrate. She hasn't moved or spoken since she collapsed, and I think she is seriously ill."

"She showed no reaction at all, except what I saw?"

"No, sir. She made no further mention of the name of

Maloney," said Nurse James. "But there is one thing you should know. I have looked through her desk and writing table, and found a letter signed by 'Al Maloney.' It was written on thin, foreign paper, undated."

"Addressed to Mrs. Liddel?" Roger asked sharply.

"Yes."

"How is the letter written?"

"As from one family to another," said Nurse James. "The handwriting is sprawling, and I would have thought it was that of an elderly man. The paper is that of the Hotel Algonquin, New York."

"Get me that letter. I'll have a man sent over to fetch it," Roger said. "Yes, at once. And keep your eyes open for the name Kane or Maloney."

"I certainly will, sir. There's one other thing — I found a receipt, nearly three years old, from Stimson's Agency — she paid them a hundred pounds. It doesn't say what for, simply for services rendered."

"That may be useful," Roger said.

Nurse James rang off, and Roger went across to Cannon Row, puzzling over the service a private detective agency had rendered for Mrs. Liddel.

He found that Maloney's affability had taken a severe drop. The three hours were up, he had not yet been released, and obviously he hadn't yet brought himself to making a protest to the American embassy. Roger had with him a typewritten version of everything Maloney had said. He handed it to the American.

"If you will agree to that, sign it as an official statement, you can go."

Relief tempered Maloney's sarcasm.

"So you really believe I can read!" He scanned the document, and held out his hand for a pen. He signed it quickly, tossed it aside, and jumped up. "I'm on my way."

"There are a few more formalities, but they won't take long." Roger picked up the statement. "Where are you going to stay tonight?"

"At Anthony Liddel's flat."

"All right." Roger nodded, and went out.

It was not until he was out of Maloney's sight that he studied the signature. "Al Maloney" was scrawled across the paper in a way that might have led some people to think that it was the signature of an older man.

Roger went slowly across to the Yard. Two cars drew up, but neither of the drivers had the letter from Nurse James. It wasn't on his desk when he reached the office. He waited, impatiently studying the signature closely, recalling the careless way in which it had been scribbled. Then footsteps approached the door, and he called "Come in!" as soon as the man outside tapped.

It wasn't the messenger; it was Detective Inspector William Sloan, tall, blond, rugged—and one of the most reliable men at the Yard.

* * * *

Roger was halfway through a summary of the case when the messenger arrived. Roger ripped open the envelope and took out the letter. But he did not need to look at the signature to compare the writing. This was a large, wavering handwriting, quite different from that of Al Maloney. He didn't think he would need expert opinion to convince anyone that two separate people called themselves by the same name.

The letter itself was a rambling recital of personal affairs, with an occasional reference to the passing of years; it was almost wistful.

15

THE SECOND "NEEDLE"

Eddie Day, the Yard's expert on forgery, looked up as Roger and Sloan entered his room, dropping a watchmaker's glass from his eyes.

"Hallo, Handsome. What-ho, Sloan—had a good time in Switzerland?"

"Fine, thanks." Sloan was very bronzed.

"Nice place—I had a week there, once. You could get plenty of francs for your pound then, it wasn't expensive like it is today. Go to Lucerne? I remember—"

"Sorry, Eddie," said Roger, "but I'm worried about this handwriting, and you're the only man who can put me right."

That was the time-honored way of winning Day's complete cooperation; he responded to flattery with pathetic regularity.

"Well, I'll try," he said modestly. "What is it?"

"Have a look at these," said Roger, and handed over the letter taken from Mrs. Liddel's flat and the statement Maloney had signed. Eddie was impulsive in everything except his own work; in that, he was painfully cautious. He examined the signatures through several different glasses, took them to a special light carefully switched on, his pointed nose almost touching the paper as he scrutinized them. He breathed noisily, through his mouth, and a gold-topped tooth glinted.

Roger drew Sloan over to a window.

"We can't hurry him. Coppell says you can come on this job with me. Care to?"

Sloan grinned; he had good teeth, and a boyish look, and he had fooled many old lags by his air of innocence.

"Why do you think I came back?"

Roger chuckled. "I had half an idea. You've heard most of what's brewing, and the A.C. talks of it as a case of needles in haystacks. The first needle was Kane. The second is Francesca. There might be a word, any time—tonight, tomorrow—about that Lancia Kane drove. Ready for an all-night session?"

"I am."

"Then when we've heard what Eddie has to say, I'll get home for a few hours. You can call me out if anything turns up."

Sloan nodded.

Eddie switched off the brighter light, and came toward them, frowning, serious, over-earnest. He handed both papers to Roger.

"Different people," he announced. "The letter was written by a man of sixty or so, no doubt about it. The signature on the statement is that of a younger man. Can't be any doubt about that either. Two different people with the same name, that's what you've found. Bad luck."

"It could be good," said Roger. "Thanks, Eddie. You may have to swear to this."

"Don't you worry," said Eddie Day.

* * * *

Roger had another undisturbed night, yet woke with a feeling of dissatisfaction. To try to disperse it, he telephoned the Yard before getting dressed. Sloan had gone off at half-past six. Evans had taken over, and would call if any word came of the Lancia.

No new reports had come in that interested him. A request to New York for information about the older Maloney might yield results, though it was unlikely; there was the hotel notepaper of the letter to Mrs. Liddel, but no envelope, nothing that could help them to say when the letter had been posted or where the writer lived.

He would check New York.

Just after ten o'clock, Sloan came in, bright-eyed and fresh.

"How are things?"

"Too quiet. Maloney went straight to young Liddel's flat, and neither of them moved out during the night. They were still there an hour ago." Roger tapped a report. "Kane hasn't talked. He's coming up at Bow Street, at ten o'clock. Sweeney is going to make a straight request for remand. I want to go and see Peel. Will you wait here until I get back?"

Sloan nodded.

"You might telephone Stimson's Agency, and tell them we want to know what work they did for Mrs. Liddel, three years ago," Roger said.

* * * *

Peel looked a sick man, but his face brightened when he saw Roger. He had already dictated a statement, against the wishes of his nurse and doctor. It might have helped, a day or two before. He gave a description of Kane as the man (who had met Francesca) at the Barnes house. Francesca had arrived by taxi. He had heard them talking, the man menacingly, but he himself had been attacked unawares. He could not say whether Francesca had gone there voluntarily or been kidnaped. He had seen no other men. The car outside had been a Lancia. Roger told him a little of what was happening, and was then shooed out by the nurse.

* * * *

Sloan greeted Roger with: "Nothing doing from Stimson's. They've changed hands in the past year, and have no back records about the Liddel woman. None of the staff did work for her, and the original Stimson is dead."

"Pity," said Roger.

"I'm just off to Bow Street," Sloan said, and went out.

The telephone rang; it was Burnaby. Roger knew that he was on duty somewhere in the case, but forgot for the moment where he was stationed. He sounded as excited as a policeman could be.

"They're going out, sir!"

"Who's going out?"

"Why, those two men—"

"Liddel and Maloney?"

"Yes, sir. I heard Liddel talking to the garage, which is in the mews, he wanted the tank filled right up and the tires checked—said he was going on a long journey."

"Delay them, if you can, until I come."

Roger's own car was parked in the Yard; he passed it, selecting a radio-equipped Humber with a supercharged engine. He told the Information Room by radio what he was doing, asking them to put out a general "watch" call for Liddel's Sunbeam Talbot or Maloney's Chrysler. He pulled up his coat collar as he drew near Hillcourt Mews.

Burnaby stood near the entrance, and gave a thumbs-up sign.

There were two ways out of the mews; the most popular was a right turn, which gave a clean run to Oxford Street. Roger pulled up at the side of the road as he heard a car engine start up nearby; it stopped again.

The Detective Officer came bustling up.

"What time were you on duty?"

"Only eight o'clock, sir."

"Get in the back, and keep out of sight," ordered Roger.

The engine was warming up again. This time, it didn't stop, and Anthony Liddel's green Sunbeam Talbot nosed its way out of the mews and turned toward Roger's car. Roger cupped his face in his hands as if lighting a cigarette, but moved off immediately afterward. Neither Maloney nor Liddel looked round; that didn't mean that they hadn't noticed him. He let them forge ahead, but kept them in sight. The green car was very noticeable.

They crossed Oxford Street, swung round Portman Square into Baker Street, and on up Park Road. Soon, they were in the St. John's Wood area, heading north. Roger kept the Yard informed by radio. As soon as he was on the Barnet By-pass, he flashed a request for a powerful car to be waiting for him at Baldock. Then he put his foot down hard, passed the green Talbot without glancing right or left, and shot ahead. They reached Baldock just after the new police car had arrived.

"Come on, Burnaby!"

Roger jumped out, and took the wheel of the other car, and called to the driver who had brought the new one:

"Get this off the road or drive in the other direction— hurry!"

He did not see the Talbot. Possibly it had taken a different turning, but if that were so, police patrols would be on the lookout for it. He drove at seventy miles an hour for five minutes, then slowed down and pulled up in a village. Burnaby was sizzling with eagerness.

"This ought to be big, sir!"

"Could be," Roger said. "Hallo, here they come."

He started off slowly as the Sunbeam Talbot came into the village. Neither Maloney nor Liddel gave him a second glance.

They were now beyond St. Neots, still heading north. Suddenly the Sunbeam Talbot turned off the main road. There was a slight hill in front of them, and Roger said:

"Watch them—see if they're moving, or just stalling."

"Right, sir." As they breasted the rise, Burnaby looked directly out of the rear window; his eyes were sharp, and he said quickly: "They've stopped—they're turning round."

"Just making sure they're not being followed," Roger said. He used the radio, asking the Lincolnshire police to have a fast car waiting for him at The George, Stamford. Burnaby fell silent for the first time, he didn't like ninety miles an hour on any road. The next car was a new 2 1/2-liter Jaguar with a good burst of speed. Roger drove through the outskirts of Stamford, with its fine buildings of Lincolnshire stone, and turned into The George, an old coaching-inn with a wide entrance arch. He left the car, and stepped to the arch, so that he could see the road but not be seen. The Sunbeam Talbot came along at steady speed, Maloney at the wheel.

Roger took the new police car from the officer in control, and drove slowly through the town.

They drove through hilly country, dotted with small clumps of trees, past sheep and grazing cattle, then across flat land. There was no need to fear that Maloney or Liddel had any idea that they were being followed. Now and again, the green car showed up in the sunlight, easily spotted by Roger, driving half a mile behind.

At the top of a hill, Burnaby exclaimed:

"They've stopped!"

The leading car was at a signpost; it was backed a few yards, and then turned right. Roger stepped on the accelerator, squealing to a standstill by the signpost. To the right, the sign read: "Little Shepton." Stuck in the hedge was another sign, with a pointing finger, which read: "Little Shepton Farm."

This road was narrow and twisting, flanked by hedges. They could see the countryside through gaps. It was flat and uninteresting; dairy country. There had been rain in the night, and the over-splash of puddles and patches of indented mud showed where the Sunbeam Talbot had passed. They came to a sharp bend and, turning, saw a farmhouse standing back from the road. It was half a mile away. A few fowls strutted about, and from somewhere came the grunting of a pig.

The green car was pulled up outside the front door; neither of the men was in sight.

Roger switched off the engine, and they coasted down the slope.

16

THE FARMHOUSE

"So we've tracked 'em down," breathed Burnaby.

Roger stopped the car two hundred yards away from the gap in the hedge that led to the farmhouse. A sign, badly in need of repainting, stuck out of a hedge. "Little Shepton Farm — Fresh Milk — Eggs."

"What are you going to do now?" The words were unnecessary, but Burnaby couldn't contain himself. "We're out of range of our radio, aren't we?"

"Yes, but there was a call out; they'll know more or less where we are."

"Just going to wait?" Waiting was the last thing Burnaby wanted.

"No. Will you go across the fields and approach from the back? Take what cover you can. All I want is to know how many people are about."

"Suits me!"

"If you're stopped say you've had a breakdown, and want to use a telephone. Call a garage, and make it sound genuine."

"Okay!"

"If you're not seen, come round to the front. If I'm not in sight, wait until I show up."

Burnaby nodded. His red face and his eyes seemed to glow.

They got out of the car, and Burnaby went back fifty yards before he came to a gap through which he could scramble. Roger went up to the main gate, keeping behind the cover of a big hawthorn bush. The house, long and low, was of gray stone with small dark windows and a slate roof. The sun had been shining over most of their route, but there were heavy clouds here, and rain threatened. There was no sign or sound at the farmhouse. The front door, shadowed by a small porch, was shut; it had once been painted brown, but now looked drab and blistered.

But for the fowls and the occasional grunting of pigs, there was no sign of life.

Roger studied the untidy garden.

It was bordered by a wire fence, and there were patches of shrubs, a few gnarled apple trees and, on one side, a farm cart that had seen better days. Everything was dilapidated. Roger watched the windows closely, saw nothing to suggest that he was being watched, started forward—and then retreated swiftly to the car. He took a long spanner from the tool box, wishing that he had thought to warn Burnaby to take a weapon.

He approached the farm cart obliquely. One of the bushes was only a few yards ahead. He could get behind that, and be within twenty yards of the house itself.

Then he heard men talking. The voices were coming from a partially open window on the first floor of the farmhouse.

He left the cover of the bush and ran toward the house. He reached the wall, heart thumping, filled now with misgivings.

His old fault was impetuosity. (Would he ever be able to cure himself of it?) He ought at least to have sent Burnaby back. He waited, hearing the mutter of voices, wishing that he could catch the drift of the conversation. He strained his ears for the sound of a woman's voice, but could hear no sound of one. The only likely reason for Maloney and Anthony Liddel's visit was, surely, to see Francesca, but there was no reason yet to believe that she was here.

He heard stealthy footsteps; and Burnaby appeared at the side of the house, twenty feet away from him. Burnaby passed a ground-floor window quickly, ducking low; he wasn't the fool he sometimes seemed.

"See anything?"

"Back door's shut, and no one's about outside," said Burnaby. "No dog, either."

"Burnaby, we've stuck our necks out too far. Take the car back to the main road. You may come across a police car on the prowl. If not, go to the first telephone. Call the Stamford police, report exactly where we are, and ask them to advise the Yard. We want more men here."

Burnaby's disappointment was almost ludicrous.

100

"Don't you think between us we could—"

"Get our heads cracked open—remember Peel," said Roger. "Hurry back, you'll be in at the kill all right."

"Very good, sir." Burnaby went off, glumly. Roger watched, seeing how skilfully he took cover behind anything offered; there was more in Burnaby than he had imagined. Roger waited for the engine of the car to start up; it didn't. That puzzled him. He found himself strained and over-anxious. Burnaby wouldn't walk, and couldn't start off without making some noise. He might have eased off the brakes and be pushing the car, so as to make no noise until he was out of earshot of the farmhouse.

If he himself went back to look, he would increase the risk of being seen. Every second he expected to hear the engine, but the wanted sound didn't come.

He took a step toward the gate.

A man said: "No, you don't."

He spun round. The man had stepped from the front door of the house, and was covering him with a service rifle.

* * * *

Roger saw that the man was small, dressed in rough tweeds, wore heavy farm boots and a cloth cap, which was pulled low over one side of his face. He had hunched shoulders; so hunched that he looked deformed. He also looked determined, and knew how to hold the gun. The barrel didn't quiver as it covered Roger's chest. The man's face was lean and weather-beaten.

Roger said: "Put that down."

"Come here, mister." The voice was heavily north country.

"Put that gun down!"

"Just you come here, mister," the man repeated. "I'm not joking."

"I am a police officer, and I order you to put that rifle down."

The man took a step forward, menace in the twist of his thin lips. Apart from the sound of his own breathing and the scratching of the fowls, Roger could hear nothing. He was a mile from the main road; out of sight and out of hearing of anyone passing there, and Burnaby must have been stopped at the car.

"I'll give you one more chance," the man said, his voice little more than a whisper. "Don't ask for trouble, mister."

Roger began : "I am a police officer, and I order you—"

He heard a sound behind him, soft, stealthy. He half-turned. He saw no one, but he was just in front of the corner of the farmhouse. Another assailant might be creeping up. His neck and forehead were damp with sweat. The man with the rifle moved the barrel a few inches—and squeezed the trigger.

The shot roared out.

The bullet went over Roger's head.

"I told you," the man said. "Come—"

There was a sudden scuffle of movement. Roger half-turned, catching sight of another man he didn't recognize, a man who had something in his right hand. He brought it down and struck Roger a glancing blow. He tried to turn, to grapple, but a second blow caught him on the forehead, sending him reeling against the wall. He was vaguely aware that the gunman was running forward, felt another blow on the top of the head, and pitched into blackness.

* * * *

It was still dark.

He was coming round, but was only half-conscious. Darkness was the thing that impressed him most; and pain. His head seemed to be on fire. He lay still, not conscious of thinking, but aware of fear.

There was no sound.

Darkness—silence—and the fire in his head.

He opened his eyes; and it was still dark. They hurt. He closed them again, and the pain grew easier. He began to remember what had happened, but was too dazed to reproach himself. He didn't think then of Burnaby or the two men he had followed, didn't think of Francesca or of anyone.

He did not know how long he lay there.

The pain continued to ease, but the darkness was as impenetrable as ever; he was aware, now, of a fusty smell.

The smell he might expect to find in a dungeon—or a cellar. Cellar? He remembered the farmhouse and the man with the rifle, the savage attack from behind.

He tried to sit up, then discovered that his hands were bound in front of him. He was lying on his back; that probably explained why his head hurt so much.

He tried to sit up, but it was no use. His efforts made the pain worse, and he cursed his own folly and the men who had done this thing.

After a while, he turned over on his side. They hadn't bound his legs, he could move them freely. Slowly he drew one knee up. He hardly knew how he managed it, but at last he was on his knees. The hardness of a stone floor bit into them.

He moved his right leg, put the foot firmly on the ground, and then, swaying to and fro, stood up. At last he was on both feet, shaky still, but in no real danger of falling. He steadied, and took a step forward cautiously, stretching out a leg. At the third step, his foot touched the wall. He drew the other leg up, then turned; and at last he was able to lean against the wall, his head bent slightly forward to make sure that it didn't touch.

After a while, he felt easier.

It was still pitch dark. There could be no window in this place; no glimmer of light of any kind came in. But perhaps the window was shuttered or curtained; he could move round, and find out.

How long had he been there?

For all he knew, it was nighttime; he had reached the farm at about half-past two.

Would he have been unconscious for several hours?

He became slowly aware of nausea in his stomach. From hunger? He forced the thought away, and moved to the right, keeping his bound hands stretched out; that was a strain on his shoulders, but there was nothing he could do about it. He grazed his fingers on brick or rough stone; no doubt, this was a cellar. The fusty smell grew stronger and the sense of nausea worsened.

He reached a corner, turned it, and went along the next wall; that was also blank. So was the third wall. Then he came upon a break in the rough surface, his fingers ran across something that was comparatively smooth; as wood. He moved his arms up and down, and touched a handle. Yes, this was a door.

He stood by it, so that he had only to stretch out his arms to touch the handle.

He moved his fingers, trying to get at the cord at his wrists, but failed; there was no chance of freeing himself by untying the cords, and he had felt nothing on which he could rub the bonds until they frayed. He waited for what seemed an age but was probably only a few minutes. He heard no sound except his own breathing, and the thumping of his heart.

He touched the handle again.

He was able to grip it, and twist. It moved. He felt a sickening sense of mingled hope and fear; the door might not be locked. He turned the handle to its full extent, and then pulled.

The door opened.

It struck his forehead, and pain shot through him, slowly subsiding. He faced the silent darkness that lay ahead. Stretching out his right leg he felt the door and eased it wider open. He knew that he was looking into a passage or into another room, but could see nothing.

He stepped forward, one pace at a time, and after two paces touched an impenetrable surface; so this was a passage.

Should he turn right or left?

He turned left—and soon came upon the same thing. He turned round slowly and painfully, and started back the way he had come, brushing the wall with his side all the time. After an age, he reached another open space. His feet kicked against stone, but his hands touched nothing. He stopped to consider, and realized that he was at the foot of a flight of steps.

He began to go up them.

Groping, he found no handrail on either side—nothing but brick or stone wall, rougher than those of the cellar. He went up a step at a time, counting. He reached seven—and knocked against a wall, and his head seemed to shriek in protest.

There was a wall behind him, too.

He turned to the right, and found more steps. He began to climb them, and when he had reached the fourth he saw a crack of light ahead.

* * * *

Roger stood swaying, filled with a strange relief. There was the outline of a door, and a slender line of light at the foot. There could be no mistaking the shape. The light was pale yellow; that of a lamp, he considered. He was on a level with the bottom of the door, so had several steps to mount. He took them cautiously.

He reached the top of the steps.

They seemed bright, compared with the darkness from which he had come. He could see the stone walls and the floor. The door itself was perhaps two yards in front of him. Would the handle be on the right or the left? He tried the right, and touched the handle. It gave him absurd pleasure, as if he had accomplished something really worth doing.

He turned the handle, and pulled, hoping desperately that the door would be unlocked. It didn't open at once. He pulled again, with almost petulant annoyance; why should it stick, why be obstinate at the time when he most needed help from inanimate things? It still refused to move. He pulled again—tugged, and strained his arms and his shoulders—but the door wouldn't budge.

Disappointment came over him like a wave from the sea. He began to shiver, and gave himself up to an orgy of angry resentment, but that soon passed. He was behaving like a child—he, Superintendent Roger West, of New Scotland Yard! He had a mind; why didn't he use it? He had no need to panic. It was the darkness and the silence—and now the dim yellow light, and the locked door. With a picklock, he could open it in a few seconds. But he hadn't a picklock, hadn't even a knife. And if he had, he couldn't get either of them out. At least, there was light. He drew back a pace, forcing himself to keep steady. Then he raised his hands, and banged on the door with his clenched fists. The sound was loud—startlingly loud—and the door shook. He banged again.

He heard footsteps.

He drew back, heart in mouth. He hadn't the least idea what to expect, knew only that someone was in the lighted room beyond. He heard a key turn in the lock—but the door seemed a long time opening. It opened at last—toward him. It struck his foot. He drew his foot away quickly, as light flooded out. Against it, tall and shadowy, Francesca Liddel was standing.

17

TWO PRISONERS

Francesca stood back, hands raised to her breast. Her face being against the light hindered him from seeing her clearly, but he had no doubt who she was. Now that he was with someone else, the dread hours of loneliness past, exhaustion overtook him. He swayed to one side, unable to save himself, fighting to keep on his feet.

Francesca sprang forward, and gripped his arms.

He grinned, foolishly: "Sorry," he said.

Keeping a firm hold of him she led him into the room. He could see that it was small; a kind of kitchen. It was warm, too. He staggered across to a table, and collapsed on the corner of it. Francesca let him go, and closed the door, locking it again. Then she stood with her back toward it.

"Mr.—West."

"Odd place to meet," Roger said. He moistened his lips. "Mind untying these cords?"

It was thick cord, really thin rope, knotted very tightly.

"Just a minute," said Francesca.

She turned to a cupboard. Something clattered as she opened a drawer. She turned again, with a carving knife in her hand, glinting in the light. Roger shivered involuntarily as she came forward and began to cut at the rope. It was tough; a few strands fell aside, but there was a great deal still to do. She stopped.

"Harder," said Roger.

"I might cut—"

"Never mind, get me free."

She began again. It was impossible to get the blade between his flesh and the rope, she had to cut downward. Twice she cut the heel of his right thumb; blood welled up. She tightened her lips, but didn't let that stop her. All the strands were severed at last, and the rope fell.

"Thanks."

But the pain was worse; his wrists seemed on fire. There were deep ridges where the rope had bitten into them, and swollen patches between. He stood there in agony while the blood poured back into his veins; it was too acute for him to move his fingers or his wrists.

He felt faint.

That passed, and he began to move his wrists gently; it was like pins and needles, caused by giant pins, giant needles. Needles! He thought of Coppell, grinned, and started to laugh. He knew that he shouldn't be laughing, but couldn't help himself. Francesca's face seemed to go round in circles; so did the room. Abruptly, her face disappeared. He felt pressure at his shoulder. She helped him off the table and led him, light-headed, toward a chair. She made him sit down, and the sudden relaxation brought blessed relief. He would have known comfort, but for the fire in his wrists. She moved away, and when she came back she had a cup in her hand. She put it to his lips.

Something cold and semisweet and rather thick — creamy *milk*. He swallowed a little, then took a gulp. Some of the milk spilled. She took the cup away.

"You'll be all right," she said.

"I — I am all right." The milk had tasted wonderful, his mouth was no longer parched. He closed his eyes. While they were closed, he felt gentle pressure at his wrists; it hurt, but the fire had died down. She was massaging them. It wasn't long before they were better; still speckled with points of fire, but bearable. For the first time he was able to look at her clearly.

She was made-up beautifully and wore a handsome green suit and blouse. Her hair clung in dark waves about her head. She had, he noted again, lovely eyes. Why should he sit here, thinking about loveliness? She drew back, then went to a stove. It was an old-fashioned iron stove, black and dirty. A fire glowed red between the bars, and he saw a kettle, even heard it singing. She poked the fire noisily, and a shower of embers fell into the pan beneath. Then she went across to the dresser.

He hadn't noticed that before. He made himself study the room, and not the girl.

It was a kitchen, too small to be in the farmhouse, he thought. The ceiling was low and discolored. The walls had been distempered green, but needed another coat badly. There were damp patches in the corners. The Welsh dresser was shiny with age. Willow-pattern crockery was placed on it, and various-colored jugs and cups hung from hooks. There were two drawers.

The corner cupboard, from which she had taken the knife, had books above it.

There were two easy chairs, of the old-fashioned saddle-back type, like that in which he was sitting. The arms were worn. There was brown linoleum on the floor, and an old-fashioned handmade wool rug of many colors, in front of the fire. By the chair opposite him was a small table.

There were two old prints on the walls—a Last Supper and a Crucifixion scene, each badly faded. There was another door, too, and one window, boarded up.

He looked back at Francesca, who was cutting bread.

The kettle was boiling.

She picked up a teapot, went across and made tea, then took it back to the dresser. Next, she carried a tray to the table, and set it down. There were sandwiches, bread and butter, cheese, and some ham; not as pink as ham usually is.

"I expect you're hungry," said Francesca.

"I am rather."

"Will you come to the table, or shall I bring the tray there?"

"Oh, I'll come." He got up. Using pressure on his wrists wasn't so good, but he managed without flinching. Francesca drew a high-backed chair to the table, and sat opposite him; there were two cups.

"Not hungry?" Roger asked.

"I've had supper."

"Pity." The bread was new, the butter luscious. the ham

hadn't the usual flavor; he could see now that it was home-cured.

Francesca poured out tea. She had an unnatural calm, but he could sense the tension behind that calmness. It showed in her eyes, in the tautness of her hands as she held the teapot; and when she pushed a large cup of tea toward him, it shook perceptibly.

Suddenly, he put his hand to his pocket, for his watch; it wasn't there. He felt in his other pockets; all of them were empty, even his wallet had been taken.

"What do you want?" asked Francesca.

"To get my hands on certain gentry, but for the moment, to know the time."

She glanced at a wristwatch.

"Ten minutes past eleven."

"Is it, by George! Er—" He found himself smiling. "You wouldn't know what day it is, would you?"

"Saturday."

"At least I haven't lost a day."

"How long had you been down there?"

"The last thing I remember was just after two o'clock this afternoon."

"No wonder you were hungry," said Francesca.

"You could have let me out before."

"I didn't know you were there."

Was there any reason to believe that she was lying, or needed to lie?

"I haven't been here all day," she went on. "They let me out for a few hours this afternoon—for the first time," she added bitterly.

"For the first time since when?"

"Monday."

"Did Kane bring you here?"

Francesca started and colored. Her voice was calm and her poise remarkable, but signs of strain were clearly visible.

"I know Kane," Roger said. "He's awaiting trial for attacking a policeman, among other things. Did you know about that?"

"I knew—he'd attacked someone. No, he didn't bring

me. He took me away from the house at Barnes. Then someone else drove me up here, on Monday night. I—" She hesitated. "I was taken to the cellar. Where you were."

"You kept very chic through it all," he said drily.

She colored again.

"They brought me some of my things, on Wednesday. I was only in the cellar for a few hours. They—they tried to frighten me."

"Why?"

"They wanted information from me."

"What information?"

She closed her eyes and went on wearily: "I don't know. They were still after the papers which they once thought they would find at Tony's flat. They still thought I knew where they were. I think I convinced them that I don't know anything about them. On Tuesday they let me come up here. I've been here ever since, except for this afternoon, when they took me for a walk. I needed that walk," she added with feeling.

"How many are there of them?"

"I've seen three."

"Did you know them before?"

"No. Two of them belong here, I think, the third man comes from London. He's short and dark. He hasn't been here all the time, but he came back today." She shivered. "I thought something was the matter, or they wouldn't have let me out."

"I was the matter," said Roger. "You knew it was Kane who attacked you and your brother, did you?"

Francesca didn't answer. Roger finished his supper, feeling better, much better. Francesca poured him out another cup of tea, and he took it to the armchair, then groped absently in his pockets for cigarettes. She took a packet from her handbag, and he lit up.

"So they let you have everything you want?"

"Food and drink and cigarettes—yes."

"Haven't they questioned you again since the first night you came?"

"No—the man from London does the questioning."

"And all he was anxious to know was about those documents?"

Francesca leaned forward in her chair, and said with great deliberation: "Mr. West, I have told you everything I can about what happened. I am not lying."

"There's plenty you haven't told me." Roger's gaze roamed round the room.

The ceilings and the walls seemed solid, but there might be a spy hole in the door. There might, also, be a gap between door and frame, through which the sound of voices would travel. Probably someone was listening to them; at least, he had to assume there was a risk of that. And if he was being observed, there were certain things that would be expected of him.

Francesca sat tight-lipped, watching him, half-afraid of what he was going to say next. She could stay afraid for a while.

He stood up.

"What are you going to do?" Francesca asked sharply.

"Look round. Didn't you know that we have to get out of here?"

"We can't," she said. "The door's locked from the outside, the window is shuttered from the outside. And I believe that someone is always watching."

"They can't watch in the dark. They probably don't think there's any risk of escape." Roger went to the door and examined it; the lock was a new mortice, and would be extremely difficult to force. He could imagine that it had been installed for just such an emergency as this. He pulled up a chair, and stood on it. There was a gap of over half an inch between the door and the frame; words could be heard outside all right. He saw nothing resembling a spy hole. He scanned the rest of the walls, then gave special attention to the dresser—and as he looked up and down it, he thought he saw something move.

He stopped abruptly.

Francesca stood up.

Roger searched the panels of the dresser, then saw a large knothole in the wood, an inch in diameter. He saw that the edges looked as if they had been freshly cut, and daubed with a stain to match the rest of the dresser. He got down from the chair, and went across to the fireplace.

III

"What did you see?" demanded Francesca, and her voice was unsteady.

"I don't know that I saw anything." He sat back in the chair, and glanced as if casually toward the hole in the dresser. He'd made no mistake, there was an eye on the other side of the hole. He gave no sign that he had realized that, but stretched out his hand.

"May I have another cigarette?"

She gave him a packet, and a box of matches.

"Thanks. Now, we'll go back a bit. Why did you go to see Kane at the Barnes house?"

"He sent for me."

"And you went, like an obedient child."

"I thought it was wise to go." In spite of what had happened and in spite of the obvious danger, there were still things that she meant to keep back.

"What happened?"

"He persuaded me to leave with him, and to come here. I didn't know that I was actually coming to this place."

"You knew he'd attacked someone?"

"He left me in an empty room for a few minutes. I heard someone cry out."

"Why were you so biddable?"

She kept silent.

Roger said: "Kane could make you do practically everything he wanted. He would call, and you would run to do his bidding. You even allowed him the run of your flat in London, when you were in America. Yet he isn't the type you would expect to mix with, is he?"

Francesca moistened her lips.

"Blackmail's a nasty thing. Why was he able to blackmail you?"

She closed her eyes.

Roger said roughly: "The innocent stuff won't get you anywhere, Miss Liddel. This is an ugly case. Murder, attempted murder, violence, gunplay – and it all revolves round you and your family. Kane blackmailed you. What did he have on you, to make it so easy?"

She kept silent; in spite of the pressure of the circumstances, even after several days of misery and fear, she could still be stubborn. He watched her closely, and knew that it wasn't going to be easy to make her talk. Did he want her to? Did he want the watching and listening men to know the truth?

But they already knew the secret that made her a victim of blackmail; no harm could come from forcing that.

"Let's have the truth," he rasped, and stood up. "Your father will be hanged, others may be killed, if you keep it back any longer. Why did you let Kane do whatever he liked? Why did you go to America? What papers was Kane after? Why—"

He stopped abruptly.

It wasn't because of the way she sat, head against the back of the chair, eyes closed, face drawn. It was because he saw something else move. She was between him and the door, and he caught sight of the movement without at first realizing what it was. Then he smelled something sharp, acrid—and the sight and sound merged together.

Smoke was creeping beneath the door.

18

SMOKED OUT

Francesca did not open her eyes, and presumably did not know what was happening. Roger drew back, staring at the smoke. Now he could smell burning.

Francesca opened her eyes.

"It's no use," she said. "I can't—" She broke off and started up. "What's the matter?"

She stood up, stumbling against him, clutched his arm, and looked toward the door. They stood close together as the smoke curled in and upward, creeping along the floor and up the walls. The smell was much stronger.

Roger relaxed.

"So that's it. We oughtn't to be surprised."

Francesca breathed: *"Fire."*

"That's right. Fire, smoke, suffocation, charred bones—that's where you've led us." Roger swung round, picked up a chair and raised it above his head, and strode to the window. The period of inaction now seemed like wasted years. He smashed at the wooden shutters, aiming at the middle. The blow jarred his wrists; never mind his wrists. He smashed again, but made no impression on the wood. At the third blow, he hesitated. Wood? The resistance was so strong it seemed more like metal. He had dented the surface, no more.

He struck again, and a leg of the chair fell off.

He dropped the rest of it, swung round, and called:

"Is there a poker? Axe? Hammer?"

The only poker was about eighteen inches long, useless for such a job as smashing down the shutters or breaking through a door. The only solid piece of movable furniture was the table, and that was too heavy to use.

Francesca was opening the cupboard; she found nothing. Roger looked beneath the dresser, but found no suitable tool. The only hope was at the door; if he could force that lock, he might be able to get out. He searched among the cutlery; there were some metal meat skewers, the only things likely to help him. He moved across the room, but the smoke was thicker, and he started to cough. He fought the spasm down, and thrust a skewer into the lock; it was useless, he knew it wouldn't work until it had a bent end; and even then, it was probably too thick. He swung round, took the skewer to the fireplace and thrust it between the bars, then levered it. When he finished he had a piece about an inch long bent at right angles.

He hardly noticed Francesca.

"Take this," she said, holding out a dampened cloth. He put it across his mouth, and she tied it at the back of his head; he could breathe through it, and there was less danger from the smoke. But it got at his eyes, and they began to sting. He touched the wood of the door, and it seemed hot.

He could imagine what it was like on the other side: a roaring furnace. He didn't know how far it was from this room to a window; if the rest of the house was ablaze he probably couldn't get through, anyway, even if he managed to break the lock.

The skewer went in again; but he knew that it was useless. He might have succeeded if he'd had more time, but this was an expert cracksman's job.

He drew back, and went to the window, tapping the shutter with the poker; the dull sound proved that the wood was either very solid or metal lined. There was no fastening of any kind inside, the shutters stretched right across the outside.

He called: "Miss Liddel!"

She didn't answer.

He turned, looking round. She had opened the door leading to the cellar. Smoke filled the room, weaving and curling about them, but outside it seemed clearer. If they went down to the cellar there was a faint hope the fire would burn itself out before they died; if they stayed in the room there was none.

The stairs loomed darkly as he and Francesca groped their way down, step by step.

He lit a match, but it burnt out almost immediately.

Francesca was close to him; he felt her hand touch his. Her fingers were icy.

"Do you think—" Her voice quivered.

"We've a chance if we stay here. Might try to block up the door with rags." He ought to have done that before. "Come on." He lit another match and led the way out of the cellar, but when they got to the top of the stairs, the smoke was so thick that both of them began to cough and choke.

They reached the kitchen—

It was a mass of red-tinged smoke.

Francesca, still holding his hand, tightened her grip.

Blocking the gaps at the door would have delayed the end, at most. Now that the fire had a good hold, it would burnt down all the wood—they couldn't keep the smoke out—and there was no exit for it, from here.

There *must* be.

He said hoarsely: "We're going to look round again. You strike the matches. Make each one last as long as you can." He gave her the matches, and they went down to the cellar again. Now that she released his wrist, he realized how tight and painful her grip had been. She was calm enough, and struck a match at the first try. She held it high; they walked round the cellar slowly, seeing nothing in the way of an escape hole—until suddenly the flickering light fell on a lighter-colored patch.

Francesca cried: "Look!"

"Another mat——" Roger began, and then a fit of coughing caught him. By the time he had recovered, the second match was nearly burnt out, but sufficient light came from it to show what they were looking at.

There had been a hole in the wall; it had been blocked up and cemented over.

Francesca began to cough, a racking, retching sound that would not stop. Roger took the matches from her, and tried again, searching the ceiling this time; and he came upon another patch, cemented in; that had been the original entrance to the cellar from outside. They were sealed off.

He said: "We'll have to try to get through."

They wouldn't get through, they would be devoured by the flames, killed in seconds, whereas it would take long minutes – hours? – to suffocate. He took her arm firmly and they began to walk out of the cellar. The flames were shooting through the door of the kitchen, and halfway down the stairs. They stood still, the heat scorching their faces.

Francesca said: "We can't." He only just caught the words. She began to cough again. Even though she was standing by his side, her face was seen as through a thick mist. Her eyes were wide open and reflecting the bright flames.

Their helplessness sickened him. The futility of it appalled him. They were at the mercy of the fire, and there was no chance to get out; no chance at all.

If they plunged forward, it *would* be over quickly.

If they waited here they might have a chance; but lingering death was much more likely.

He looked at Francesca, standing motionless against the red-tinged smoke; and he did not see Francesca, but an image of Janet.

* * * *

Detective Inspector William Sloan no longer looked boyish or ingenuous. The local Superintendent, with him in the office at the Stamford police headquarters, had never seen a man look more savage or more ruthless.

"They're somewhere in the district," Sloan said. "Both cars were reported as far as Stretton, and then they disappeared. They must be here."

The local man said, "We've searched everywhere, Inspector, and haven't found either of the cars."

Sloan turned to a map stretched out on the Superintendent's desk, already marked with pencil lines. He traced the town where the cars had been seen, and studied the map closely.

"Could have taken any one of a dozen or more turnings," said the Superintendent. "May be miles away by now. Every man I can get hold of is searching, and we've a lot of voluntary help. The moment we get a lead, we'll move. And there may not be any immediate danger."

The telephone rang. Both men snatched at it, Sloan got it first, then let it go. The Superintendent, a thin, rakish-looking man, put the receiver to his ear.

"Superintendent Mellish speaking."

There was a pause, but not a pause in tension. Sloan saw the way the other's hand tightened, saw the sudden glint in his eyes.

"*Where?*"

Sloan held himself absolutely rigid.

"Little Shepton Farm—yes, I know it." Mellish banged down the receiver, and shouted: "Palmer!" A sergeant came in quickly. "Little Shepton Farm. Get all cars converging on it. I'm going straight away. Come on, Sloan." He ran out of the office, to the steps of the police station, Sloan close on his heels. His car was waiting in the road, and he was at the wheel within sixty seconds of putting down the receiver.

Sloan slid in beside him.

"How far?"

"Eleven miles—good road."

"What's the report?"

"Three men, including your man Burnaby, were found at the farm twenty minutes ago. None of them is badly hurt. West was there early this afternoon, but isn't there now."

Sloan grunted, and lit a cigarette. The Superintendent

drove on his horn and his brakes, and policemen in the town waved him on. Once on the open road, he let the car all out.

In the west, to their right, was a pale-red glow in the sky.

Sloan said: "Right or left?"

"Right."

"Over there—that glow?"

The Superintendent glanced toward it, and said: "Looks like a fire."

"Your people are at the farmhouse, aren't they?"

"Should be."

They swerved to avoid a heavy milk truck with a trailer, were vaguely aware of the driver shouting at them. The Superintendent kept his headlights on, and they passed two signposts. The glow of the fire grew brighter, and smoke hid the stars. They drew nearer another signpost, and Mellish said:

"I think this is it."

The headlights caught the signpost and the words: "Little Shepton." How they missed the hedge as they swung round, Sloan would never know.

The fiery glow was almost straight in front of them, and they slowed down. Men appeared at the hedges, waving them on. They breasted a low hill, and then looked down at the fire and the scene about it. The glow spread for miles, and they could see the skeleton framework of the blazing cottage. They could also see the cars clustered near it—and others, near another house, on the left.

"It's one of the farm cottages," the Superintendent said. "Not much water about here."

There was no fire engine in sight.

They went past the farmhouse, and stopped near the cars. The heat struck at them. Sloan jumped out, and a policeman in uniform came forward. Smoke made Sloan choke, muffling the man's words.

"What was that?"

"Not a hope of saving the place or anyone in it," the local man repeated. "They're getting as near as they can, though they haven't seen any sign of anyone yet. It may be an empty cottage. There used to be an entrance to the cellar from outside, but it's blocked up. If anyone was in there, they'd probably go to the cellar. I've sent for pickaxes."

Sloan said: "Where's this entrance?"

"It's a bit hot close by, sir."

"Where is it?"

The policeman led the way, the Superintendent went along with Sloan. It was searingly hot, but the wind was blowing away from them, and they were able to draw near. There was an entrance to a disused chute; feeding-stuff had once been kept in the cottage cellar, and the chute used for stocking it up. The entrance itself was about twenty feet from the wall of the house. As they reached it there was a loud blast, pieces of stone flew in all directions, staggering the gasping men. There was another roar as part of the wall caved in.

The policeman's face was bleeding.

"I'm all right, sir."

The entrance to the chute had been filled up with cement. Sloan rapped at it with his heel, but met only solid resistance. Round him the heat burned relentlessly in to his body. The uncertainty was almost worse, in its way, than irrefutable knowledge. Roger might be there—might already be among that burning mass.

A car came up, and men jumped out, pickaxes began to swing. Sparks flew up and from the cement, chippings flew in all directions. Another part of the cottage wall caved in, and burning stones cascaded toward them. One man fell, with a wound in his leg. Sloan grabbed his pickaxe.

Other men were digging round the cement, and one man called out:

"I'm through!"

He was pulling at the point of his pickaxe, with an effort. Others joined him, and began to attack the weak spot. The red glow and the headlights of the cars showed everything clearly—grotesque figures of sweating men as they flung themselves into the attack.

The hole grew larger.

A man tossed his tool away, and said in a hoarse voice:

"I can get down there now, I reckon."

He didn't ask for approval, but lowered himself into the chute, and disappeared.

19

SOME ANSWERS

"He ought to have had a rope," Sloan said. "Any here?"

Another man came forward.

"Plenty." He was tying a rope round his waist.

"I want to go down," Sloan said abruptly.

"Too big, sir—you'll only get wedged." The man tossed the rope to another, and followed the first down the chute. As he disappeared, there was a shout, which might have meant anything or nothing. The man holding the rope said:

"Better get ready to pull, they'll suffocate mighty quickly."

Others came forward and took the rope, the Superintendent and Sloan joining them. There was another shout—and the word was distinguishable. "Pull!" They pulled, and there was a heavy weight on the end of the rope.

A woman's head; a woman's body, with the rope tied beneath her arms, and behind her, the first of the men who had ventured down. He staggered as he was helped out, and muttered almost unintelligibly:

" 'Nother one—hurry! 'nother one—hurry!"

Five minutes later, Roger and Francesca were lying side by side on the grass near the cottage, their faces seared in the glow, their eyes closed. The Superintendent was bending over Francesca, Sloan was standing and staring down at Roger. His teeth were clamped together, and stayed clamped until Mellish finished with Francesca, gave instructions to the waiting police, and then came to Roger.

"Any hope?" Sloan growled.

"Touch and go with the woman, I think." The Superintendent bent down, and began to examine Roger. He seemed to be there for an age; Sloan's teeth were gritting together so fiercely that his jaws ached.

The Superintendent stood.

"He's tougher," he observed.

* * * *

At the Bell Street house Mark Lessing sat in Roger's chair, while Janet stood by the window, looking out; the curtains were drawn back. It was nearly one o'clock. The last news had come through just after twelve, and that had really been no news. All they knew was that Roger had been missing since early afternoon.

Janet turned round. Her eyes were glassy, her face hadn't a touch of color.

"Let me get you a drink," Mark said.

"No, thanks. Mark, it couldn't happen like this, could it?"

"Of course it couldn't! Roger's been in plenty of tight places."

"That's just it." Janet's voice was low, colorless. "There'll be one he doesn't get out of. I've been scared ever since the attack on Peel. And I've always thought it would come when we didn't really expect it. Suddenly." She raised clenched hands. "How I hate his job!"

"We'll get news," Mark said.

Janet didn't speak, but he saw tears flooding her eyes. She flung herself out of the room, and he heard her going up the stairs. To the boys' rooms, of course. He thought it better that she should be alone. As he stood up the telephone rang.

He snatched at it, and knocked it off the table. He was straining to stretch the cable from the floor when Janet burst in. She stood in the doorway, scarcely breathing.

A man said: "Tell Mrs. West that everything's all right, will you?"

"Hurt?"

"Not seriously, he'll be as good as new in a couple of days."

"Wonderful!" cried Mark.

When he reached Janet she was crying.

* * * *

Roger's first thought when he came round was to wonder where he was; the second, to answer the first. He was in a small ward in a hospital, or nursing home. There was a faint smell of antiseptics. The square window showed a bright garden of sunlight striking the tops of trees. He smiled faintly, subconsciously contrasting this with where he had last known himself to be.

Then he thought of Francesca.

He sat up sharply. He was stiff, but could move freely. His mouth and lips were sore and his eyes were painful, but the pain wasn't excessive, he knew there was nothing seriously the matter with him. There were plasters on his hands where he had grazed them on the walls of the cellar. But how was Francesca?

On the bedside table was a thermometer, a bunch of grapes, and a bell push. He pressed the bell and picked off several grapes. He lifted them to his mouth, then put them down again. A nurse came in, middle-aged, motherly, gray-haired.

"Good morning! How are you feeling?"

"All right, thanks." He kept his voice steady. "There was a lady with me."

"Yes, she's in the next ward," the nurse said. "She hasn't recovered so quickly as you, but she'll be all right. She's sleeping quite normally now."

Roger felt an enormous wave of relief. "That's wonderful!"

"I'll ask the doctor to come to see you."

The doctor was young, slight of build, a miniature Greek god, with a pleasant manner and mellow assurance in his voice. The wise thing was for Roger to stay where he was for today.

"I've telephoned the police station, where another Scotland Yard officer is waiting," said the Greek god. "I'd see him first, if I were you."

"There's no harm in that," Roger said.

Sloan arrived half an hour afterward, buoyant, almost boisterous, and more boyish than ever. He had only a few scratches to show for the night's excitement. There was a small armchair, and he sat back and stretched his legs out comfortably.

"And why so happy?" Roger demanded. "Is everything sewn up?"

"Not by a long way! But compared with what I thought

would happen last night, everything's wonderful. Janet phoned and asked me to send the grapes. She wanted to come up, but I told her there was no need."

"Did she know—"

"She had a bad hour or two, that's all." He paused, then added: "Francesca Liddel came off worse than you, but she'll be able to talk in a day or two."

"If we can find a way of making her talk," Roger said. "Let me have the story as far as you know it, will you? How did you find us?"

"That's chiefly due to a certain Mr. Maloney," Sloan said, and chuckled. "That shake you?"

"I'm not yet convinced," Roger said, heavily.

Sloan shrugged. "I don't pretend that he's in the clear, but he was tied up with Burnaby and Anthony Liddel at that farmhouse, and managed to free himself. He released the others and staggered out, and one of the searching policemen found him. That brought us to the cottage. The local people are checking on the farmer, and will give us a full report. For the rest . . ."

Roger listened carefully.

* * * *

Roger reached London soon after lunchtime, spent a couple of hours at home with Janet, and then went to the Yard. He read through the various reports, about which Sloan had told him. A full report was to follow about the men who lived at the farm—both named Harring. Roger telephoned to the hospital for a report on Francesca, who was making steady progress. He looked through the newspapers, which had splashed the story heavily, but there was nothing useful in any of them. Kane still refused to talk. None of the three men who had been at Little Shepton Farm had been caught. The two cars had been found in a wood, a few miles away—undamaged.

The door opened, and Coppell loomed in.

"Well, Handsome?"

"Hallo, sir."

"You're not looking too bad."

"Except for a swollen throat and some stiffness, I'm all right."

"Lucky you!"

"Yes, I know I asked for it," Roger said. "I've been looking through the reports."

"What do you make of them?" Coppell sat on a corner of the desk, towering massively over Roger, who shifted his chair as near the wall as it would go.

"That we haven't the main answer yet, which is obvious. That the man from London Francesca Liddel talked about replaces Kane as the danger on the other side. That Francesca Liddel had admitted being blackmailed, but hasn't yet explained why. That the whole family appears to have been blackmailed, at one time or another. That Francesca had a special mission to the United States, and hasn't told us what it was, and that Al Maloney isn't all he seems to be."

"A nice lot of negatives," Coppell observed. "There's some news from the States. They've traced a young Al Maloney to a New York hotel, and uncovered the fact that Francesca Liddel met him there. Does that help?"

"I'm going to see Liddel and Maloney now," said Roger.

* * * *

Maloney opened the door of the Hillcourt Mews flat. He had a patch of plaster over his right eye, and the left one was purple, but his grin was there, and obviously he had identified Roger from the window.

The sitting room was empty.

"Where's Liddel?" asked Roger.

"Being filial, and visiting his mother. She had a relapse. Someone told him it was after a visit from you, and so he's breathing vengeance."

"If he'd breathe just a little sense, it would help. The same applies to you. Why did you go north?"

"My, my!" exclaimed Maloney, his grin broadening. "Can't *you* read! I've told three policemen already and signed a statement."

"I want to know the truth," Roger said. He sat on the arm of a chair, and accepted a Camel from a battered packet.

"You know the truth, Superintendent! We had a

message saying if we went to this place, we would find Frankie. That's what we told you we were going to do. Maybe we were fools to go alone, but we'd been told not to parley with policemen. That man knew a thing or two. Do you still imagine that Frankie went off on her own accord?"

Roger said clearly: "I don't know."

Maloney backed a pace, and frowned. His expression was strained and anxious.

"What in hell are you saying? Frankie nearly died. Another half an hour, and I guess she would have been dead. Think she did that herself?"

"Accidents happen. I've no proof that she had been kept there against her will."

"You're crazy!"

"The crazy ones are those who have been fooling around without telling us why. I don't know that Francesca Liddel was kidnaped. I only know that it looks that way, and she might have built it up, to make it seem convincing—and made one fatal mistake."

Maloney growled: "What mistake?"

"Trusting a man who couldn't be trusted. A man who decided she was better out of the way."

Maloney swung round, and spoke over his shoulder.

"You're still crazy!"

"You're still suspect."

Maloney didn't look straight into Roger's eyes. He played with his tie, one of many colors.

"Didn't anyone tell you that if I hadn't found my way out of those knots, you and Francesca would be dead by now?"

"Yes, they told me."

"What am I suspected of? Saving the life of a cop who would be better dead?"

Roger said: "No one's told me how it was you happened to get free. No one's told me why the men who were supposed to have tied you up were careless with you. They weren't careless about many things. No one's told me whether you did your gallant act after you thought that Miss Liddel and I would be roasted alive. I want all the answers."

20
SUDDEN ILLNESS

Maloney strode across the room, opened a cabinet, and took out a bottle of Scotch. It was not yet twelve o'clock. He poured out half a small glass, and tossed it down, then held the bottle out to Roger.

"Drink?"

"This case started with poison—did you know? Arsenic. A man was killed with it. He thought he was eating an ordinary dinner, and someone used it as a cover for arsenic. That gave him a painful death."

"This whisky's all right."

"I wouldn't be so sure. You're mixing with dangerous people. They'll kill you as cheerfully as they'll take your money or your help. What makes you trust anyone? What makes you so friendly with Anthony Liddel?"

Maloney said: "I like him almost as well as his sister. I haven't got the answers. I fell in love with Frankie and came to help her, and from now until I break my neck, I'm going to do just that."

"I'm glad you've put a limit on it. Poison or a broken neck lead to the same-shaped coffin."

"For an English dick," said Maloney, "you use funny tactics."

"I'm telling you that either you're in this up to your neck, or else you're in line for murder."

"Wrong, both times."

"Where's Liddel?"

"Seeing his mother."

Roger said: "Mind if I use your phone?" He stretched out, plucked it off the cradle, and dialed the Maybury Crescent number. Maloney put the Scotch on a table, and thrust both hands deep into his pockets.

A woman answered: "This is Mr. Liddel's house."

"Who is that speaking?"

"Maisie, sir—Mrs. Liddel's maid."

"Mr. Anthony Liddel, please."

"Mr. Anthony? *He's* not here."

"Has he been there this morning?"

"I don't think so, sir—who is that?"

"Superintendent West. Find out if he's been, will you? I'll hold on." He watched Maloney, who didn't speak. The maid was gone for some time, and there were crackling noises on the telephone. When she came back, she sounded breathless.

"No—no, sir, he hasn't been here, but the nurse says can you come?"

"Why?"

"Madame's *very* ill again, sir—ever so ill."

"I'll come," said Roger. He rang off, but didn't move at once. Maloney found it easier to meet his eye, perhaps because of the Dutch courage not unrelated to the bottle of Scotch.

"I can't make everyone a little George Washington," Maloney said.

"You could start on yourself. Did you see your father before you left New York?"

"What a cop! I've no father."

"Your uncle."

"What is this, a personality parade?"

"A straight question—did you see your uncle before you left New York?"

Maloney strolled across to him.

"As far as I know, I haven't a relation in the world. But I'm going to have a close one soon, if I can fix it."

Roger went out. Maloney didn't move after him, and wasn't at the window when he reached the courtyard. The policeman on duty in the mews nodded. Roger beckoned him.

"Did Mr. Liddel go out this morning?"

"Yes, sir."

"What time?"

"Nine twenty-five. He went on foot—that is, he didn't take his car, he might have taken a taxi later."

"Thanks." Liddel was still out, then, not hiding in the flat; why should he hide? Why should any of the Liddels hide themselves, or anything else, even at such great risk to their lives? There had been a moment when Roger had thought that the case was nearly over. He didn't think that now. From the beginning, he hadn't been happy about it, least happy about the resigned way in which James Liddel had faced his arrest. A willing sacrifice—for what? The answer seemed to be that he was shielding someone—but whom? There was no real evidence of it, only indications, and these might have built themselves up in his own mind. As things stood, Liddel was still awaiting trial. There was fresh evidence that there had been strange happenings in the family, but none to shake the available evidence about the murder of Lancelot Hay.

Should he try to probe more deeply into Hay's life?

He hadn't found out whether Hay and Kane had crossed each other's path. That was a new angle. Hay had been a wastrel, a no-good—and so had Kane. He stopped at a telephone kiosk and called the Yard.

"I'll do what I can," Sloan said, but he sounded dubious. "It'll take time."

"You might strike lucky early. I'm going to see Mrs. Liddel, I'm told she's had another relapse."

"Want any help?"

"Have Maltby stand by, if he's about," said Roger. He trusted Maltby's medical opinion above most people's, and Mrs. Liddel's private doctor had a bias against the police.

In the morning sunlight, the houses in Maybury Crescent looked pleasing in their symmetry. There was stateliness in them, a suggestion of well-being; this was a residential backwater, in which commerce and the professions had not yet penetrated. The brasses outside Number 11 shone, and the green door glowed; it had been painted within the past few months, before there had been any shadow of dark events.

But in this, Roger corrected himself; the blackmail had preceded those events, was most probably the cause of them—and that had been going on for years. Lancelot Hay had often come into this house.

Roger rang the bell, and the door opened almost before his finger came off the bell push. The maid, Maisie, was no longer calm, but gray-faced; alarmed. She backed away, hands at her flat breasts, breathing heavily, just as she had been when she had come to the telephone.

"The doctor's with her, sir, oh she's *terribly* ill."

Roger ran up the stairs. He saw the door of the bedroom ajar; that puzzled him, until Nurse James came hurrying from another room, carrying a bucket. The nurse looked strained. She didn't speak, but nodded toward the room. He heard a sound of retching, and went in.

The nurse had hurried to the bedside. Mrs. Liddel was sitting up, her face distorted. The doctor stood over her. He was fitting up a contraption that was familiar enough to Roger—a stomach pump.

The nurse slipped unobtrusively past Roger, lowering her voice: "This started this morning, about ten o'clock. It's been terrible. I don't know whether we shall save her."

"Anyone been to see her?"

"I don't think—"

"Hurry, nurse," said the doctor testily. He looked up, started, and waved Roger away. The nurse joined him. Roger went out, thinking of all the implications.

Lancelot Hay had died, after such symptoms as these, of arsenic poisoning.

Roger heard Maisie walking across the hall. The front door opened, and Maltby came bustling in, looking more like a tame gorilla than ever. He caught sight of Roger at the head of the stairs, and came hurrying up.

"What's the panic?"

"More arsenic, I shouldn't wonder. They're using a stomach pump."

"Ho-ho!" exclaimed Maltby. "I'll go and lend a hand." He went in, waving abruptly as he disappeared. Roger went slowly down the stairs. Maisie was standing at the foot of them.

"She has two doctors looking after her," Roger said soothingly. "Maisie, are you sure that no one came here this morning?"

"Oh, *yes*, sir. No one's been here. Dear Mr. Anthony telephoned, and cook took the message. There's only me and cook here just now, sir, it's a big house to run for the two of us."

"I'm sure it is. Where is cook?"

"She's out shopping, she won't let *anyone* else select the fish, she always does it herself."

"Where have you been all the morning?"

"Well—"

"I only want to know what part of the house you've been in, since cook went out—how long has she been gone?"

"She went about nine-fifteen, sir. And I was upstairs, doing the bedrooms. I did Madame's very thoroughly this morning. She was looking ill and said she had pains in her stomach when I last looked in. Then when you telephoned, the nurse told me to send for you. She *will* be all right, won't she?"

"I think so. You didn't come downstairs after cook had gone?"

"No, not once."

"Show me the back door, will you?" asked Roger.

Unlike many of the houses in this part of London, this had a service road at the back, and therefore a back entrance. He was taken through spacious, modernized kitchen quarters by an agitated Maisie, who couldn't imagine what the Superintendent could be looking for.

Suddenly, he said: "Does Mrs. Liddel approve of cook smoking in the kitchen?"

"Cook *smoke?* Why, I've never heard such a thing. She won't have anyone smoke in here. I never smoke, either, sir, I don't know what you mean."

There was a cigarette butt near the big yellow Aga cooker. Without drawing attention to it, he retrieved the cigarette stub; the end was damp. It was not much more than half-smoked, and had the familiar name Players printed in pale blue. He put it in a small envelope and slipped the envelope into his waistcoat pocket, then inspected the back door. It hadn't been forced, but probably it was kept open during the day. That was something he had to check with Maisie.

At a loss for words, she quickly became indignant. Of course, cook had a key, they wouldn't dream of going out without making sure that the door was locked. Mr. Liddel had always been most strict about that, and so had Mrs. Liddel.

"Who has a key to the back door?" Roger asked.

"Well, sir, there's me and cook, and Johnson, the butler,

when he's at home; he's had to go away because of some illness in his family."

"And who else?"

"Well—*all* the family, of course, and Mr. Hay had one."

"A back-door key?"

"The garage is near the back entrance, just at the end of the alley, and they often came in the back way," Maisie said. "I do wish I knew why you were asking all these questions, Mr. West; I'm sure I've done nothing I shouldn't, but I don't know whether I ought to answer." She was almost in tears.

He reassured her, gently. "Let me have your key, will you?"

She surrendered it without protest.

He heard a door opening upstairs. Maltby came hurrying down, waving Maisie away.

"Well?" Roger almost barked the word.

"Oh, we've saved her."

"Arsenic?"

"I'll tell you definitely in a couple of hours, but I'll be surprised if it isn't. The symptoms all add up. The family G.P. upstairs doesn't want to admit it, says it could be extreme nervous reaction following the series of shocks, but I think you can rule that out. It's arsenic or some other irritant poison. If she hadn't been under that nurse's care, we might have been too late. You know, Handsome, I don't think you've found Lancelot Hay's murderer yet."

"You could be right," Roger conceded. He looked through the house, stopping for some minutes in the darkroom on the half-landing. He poked about, but found nothing of fresh interest.

He left with Maltby, after telephoning the Yard for two men to stand by. He did not drive to the Yard, but to Liddel's flat. The green Talbot was outside the garage, but neither of the men was there. Roger went up the stairs; this time, it was Anthony Liddel who opened the door. They went into the living room.

"Having a busy morning?" Liddel asked.

Roger said: "How was your mother when you saw her?"

"I haven't seen her. I decided that I couldn't bear more grief."

"Where have you been?"

"Walking's good for one. Haven't you heard?"

"You'd better prove you walked," Roger said. "Mind showing me your keys?"

He fingered the one he had taken from Maisie, as he watched Liddel. Liddel didn't like the request, and started to protest, then shrugged his shoulders and took out the keys on his ring. His hand was unsteady. There were three Yales in all. Roger took out the one from Maybury Crescent; one of Liddel's was identical.

"So what?" Liddel asked.

"Interesting," said Roger. "Mr. Liddel, I shall ask you to swear on oath, very soon, that you did not visit your mother at her house this morning. Would you care to think again, before you answer?"

"Be damned to you, no!"

Maloney appeared in the doorway, hands in pockets, slouching, frowning.

"I'd like you to come with me," Roger said.

The words were hardly out of his mouth before Liddel smashed a blow at his face, catching him completely by surprise, and sending him reeling back. Then Liddel turned and rushed out of the room.

21

FARMHOUSE FIND

Roger, recovering, went forward, saw Maloney looming in front of him, obstructive but not aggressively so. Roger didn't pull up, and Maloney stayed where he was. Roger smashed a straight left into his stomach, saw the look of pained surprise before Maloney doubled forward. Roger pushed him away, squeezed between him and the door, and reached the hall.

The door was closed.

He shouted, but shouting wouldn't help much, the man outside should stop Liddel. A car engine started up. Roger pulled open the door. When he reached the mews, Liddel was disappearing, and the watching detective was flat on his back.

Roger called: "See which way it goes!" He went back, forcing himself not to hurry. Maloney was leaning against a chair, pressing his hands to his stomach. Roger went to the telephone and dialed 999.

"This is West. Put out a general call for Anthony Liddel, driving a green Sunbeam Talbot, registration number Z1252, now in the West End. You have a description of Liddel. Hold him for assaulting a police officer. Warn all patrols that he may be armed and violent. Understood?"

"All understood, sir."

Roger rang off. Maloney had been watching him, while gently massaging his stomach. He looked better, and his lips were twisted in a wry smile.

"You pack quite a punch," he remarked.

"Several kinds of punches," said Roger. "Another will catch up with you soon." He could go on trying to make the man talk; but it would be a waste of time. He went out, without another word.

Outside, the detective was fingering a knee.

"He turned right, sir."

"What happened to you?"

"I went to detain him, and he kicked me—caught me on the kneecap. I'd like to—"

"You'd better be relieved until you've had that seen to," said Roger. "I'll send someone. Report if Maloney leaves."

"Yes, sir."

Roger drove back to the Yard, walked briskly to his office, and found Sloan poring over files. Sloan looked up, and his eyes rounded.

"What's up?"

"Anthony Liddel on the rampage, and his mother's down with arsenic poisoning," Roger said. He rang the bell for a sergeant, who came in at once. "Have the man at Hillcourt Mews relieved, he's had a slight accident."

"Right, sir!"

Roger put down the receiver. Sloan was standing up, frowning. The office was silent, the familiar sound of traffic going along the Embankment and the whistle of an engine some way off were the only sounds. Sloan smoothed down his straw-colored hair, but didn't speak until Roger relaxed and stretched out his hand for a cigarette.

"So it's turned full circle," Sloan said. "We're back to arsenic. Think Liddel gave it to her?"

"That's the way it seems."

"So he could have poisoned his cousin Lancelot."

"Could is the word. And it's conceivable that his father knew it, and is shielding him." Roger went over what had happened, while looking at the back-door key. "I don't think there's any doubt that he was at the house and saw his mother. But there's one odd thing. He told Maloney where he was going, and Maloney told me. That doesn't argue premeditated poisoning, does it?"

"So you're not falling for the obvious," Sloan said.

"I know there's a hell of a lot we don't know," Roger said irritably. He smoked in silence for a few minutes, and then stretched out for the telephone, but he didn't lift the receiver. "You haven't found anything to suggest that Lancelot Hay and Kane were acquainted, have you?"

"No."

"Any news from the north — about the farmhouse?"

"No, not much about the farmhouse. Francesca Liddel's much better, she'll be out of hospital tomorrow."

"I think I'll go and see her today," Roger said. "Getting about in this job, aren't I?" He gave a humorless laugh. "I'm feeling very pleased with myself! I could have held Liddel, and in his frame of mind I think he would have talked. Now—" He broke off, shrugging.

"We'll pick him up," Sloan said confidently.

"I hope so." Roger lifted the telephone receiver. "Give me Detective Officer Burnaby, will you?" He held on, until Burnaby came on the line. "Burnaby, I'm going north again, and it'll be a less eventful journey. Care to come with me?"

"That's very good of you, sir — yes."

"In half an hour, then," Roger said, and rang off. "Bill, call the Stamford people for me, and tell them I'll be there this afternoon, will you? I'm going to have a look at that farmhouse in daylight, and hear about the people who owned it. I'd like to give Little Shepton Farm more attention."

"Now what's in your mind?" Sloan asked.

Roger shrugged.

"Want to know what's in mine?" asked Sloan.

"I've been waiting for that," Roger said. "You've come back fresh to it, and probably see a dozen things which I don't."

"What a hope!" Sloan waved a disclaimer. "You haven't missed anything, but you may not have seen everything quite the way I have. First, the blackmailing of James Liddel was said to be because of a love child."

Roger nodded.

"We don't know where this love child went to or what happened to him. There's a statement that it was a boy, but we don't even know that for certain. We do know that a certain Mr. Al Maloney is extremely interested in Francesca Liddel, and we also know he has no relatives."

"He could be the love child, you mean?"

"Possibly. And if he is, it could mean that the story that Maloney is in love with Francesca is hooey. That could be his excuse for his interest in the case."

"Yes," agreed Roger. "What next?"

"We want to know why Francesca went to the States," said Sloan. "Why not simply to find her half-brother? Remember, her father was being blackmailed. At the time she didn't know that the blackmailer was Lancelot Hay. She knew about a Mr. Maloney who had been writing to her mother, and she went to check that, and met young Maloney. She soon found out that he wasn't the blackmailer, because he has all the money he could want. So— perhaps she fell in love. That would explain her manner when she returned to England—why she was so strange, why she—"

"Didn't want her photograph taken?"

"I haven't got the answer to that one, but when a woman's in love, she often gets whims and fancies. And it could be true that she's always disliked being photographed. That incident might mean nothing much."

"I could believe it if she hadn't been to see Cardew of the *Record*. Well, we'll see. What else, Bill?"

"Well, if Anthony Liddel killed Lancelot, he wouldn't be above killing his mother, if—well, let's put it this way. She's highly emotional, nearly hysterical. That might be because she knows her son was the killer and seemed ready to let her husband hang for the murder he committed. Shocking situation for a woman to find herself in. Let's say that Anthony saw his mother this morning, discovered that she knew the truth, and decided to get rid of her."

"If she suspected him, would she take anything to eat from him?"

"If her breakfast tray was in the room, he could have slipped it in."

Roger said: "Yes, he *could* have done. I don't know. I'll be glad when they've picked up Liddel. We ought to have some word by now." He called the Information Room, but there was no news.

He had hardly put the receiver down before the telephone rang.

"Information Room again, sir. We've just had word that the Sunbeam Talbot has been picked up on Hampstead Heath."

"Liddel?"

"No sign of him."

Roger grunted. "Thanks." He put the receiver down and looked at Sloan. "Make that priority—get Anthony Liddel."

* * * *

Burnaby had unsuspected qualities; he was an excellent driver, and, now that there was no overriding excitement, silent and tactful. He took the wheel halfway along the road to Stamford, and drove while Roger leaned back, letting thoughts slide through his mind. He knew better than to force them at this stage. He hardly noticed the green countryside, the fields and wooded patches, or the passing traffic; or Burnaby. He pondered all that Sloan had said, all that had followed Francesca's visit to Bell Street. Somewhere in the early stages of this second part of the investigation was a clue that, when he recognized and understood it, would probably explain most of what had happened. He concentrated on Francesca's fear for her mother. If she had really been frightened, and he thought she had, it would easily be explained if she knew that her brother was the murderer.

Would she keep silent?

She was fond of her father; that seemed to be the one normal relationship in the family. If he thought it worthwhile keeping silent and making the great sacrifice, then Francesca might be persuaded to. But it wasn't satisfying; it wasn't a big enough motive. He could not bring himself to believe that father and daughter would keep silent, knowing the truth, if such truth were the only reason for their silence.

That would make it a family affair, pure and simple. It wasn't. Kane was an interloper. So was the mysterious "man from London" who had questioned Francesca at the farmhouse, and who had set the cottage on fire. It could have been Maloney or Anthony Liddel, if Francesca had lied. But while it was possible to imagine a motive for Anthony, there wasn't one for Maloney—there was no reason at all why Maloney should lend himself to this kind of intrigue simply for the sake of the family.

There was even less reason to believe that Maloney was a criminal.

There were indications, but no real evidence, that Maloney might be Francesca's half-brother.

Burnaby broke a long silence.

"We won't be long now, sir."

Roger glanced at the dashboard clock. "Half-past three—we've made good time. You enjoy driving, don't you?"

"Always had one ambition," said Burnaby, greatly daring. "I started off wanting to be a racing-car driver, and now—what wouldn't I give to be a Flying Squad driver, sir!"

Roger smiled faintly. "I'll see what can be done."

"You didn't mind me saying—" Burnaby was anxious.

"Not a bit. If you want to risk your neck, there's no reason why I should try to stop you. Married?"

"No, sir. The Force is my life."

There were many like him at the Yard.

They drove more slowly through the outskirts of Stamford, and just before four o'clock reached the police station. Both Roger and Burnaby, recognized by the man on duty, were told that the Superintendent was waiting for them, and were ushered up to his office.

"You go and get some tea, Burnaby," Roger said.

"Thank you, sir."

Superintendent Mellish was as thin-faced, deep-voiced, and hospitable as ever. Within two minutes of Roger entering the office, tea and cakes were brought in; appetizing-looking cream cakes, and Roger liked cream. The Superintendent, anxious to know how things were progressing, had little new information. He had seen Francesca Liddel that morning, and although she was actually much better, she hadn't talked.

"What about the farmhouse?" Roger asked.

"I thought we'd go and have a look over it," said Mellish. "It's owner, Fred Harring, has always been a queer stick. That's the man with the humped back, who had the gun. The man who hit you must have been his son—Matthew. The mother died in childbirth. They've never been very successful, selling the land bit by bit until now it's little more than a smallholding. They lived there together, no woman in the place, just a couple of misanthropes. They have about six hundred pounds standing to their credit. Have another cake."

"I wish your baker lived in London," Roger said. "Any information about recent visitors to the farm?"

"Rumors and facts which have come in since the fire. A farm worker who lives in a cottage a couple of miles away says he saw a car outside the farm more than once, and that the Harrings had several visitors lately. All men. He didn't get close to see them, so we can't get any description, but it's probably true. It's certainly true that the cottage was let to a man named Smith, who stayed there for weekends, and did some solitary rough shooting. More tea?"

"No, thanks, I'd like to get out to the farm. Any description of Smith?"

"Small and dark," said Mellish. "Well, I'm ready." He stood up briskly. "If you're going to bring your man, I needn't take anyone else. We're stretched to the limit for staff. Mind if we go in my car?"

Roger chuckled. "Please yourself."

The farmhouse looked exactly as he remembered it. The

fowls still scraped, and the pigs still grunted, a neighbor was looking after them, Mellish said. Half a mile away, on the slope of a hill, the charred ruins of the cottage looked black and desolate. No one was about. They took the car as near as they could, and walked to the chute. The hole had been greatly widened, and it was possible to see into the cellar. A ladder had been placed so that anyone could get down easily.

"Doesn't it give you the shivers?" asked Burnaby.

"Not yet," said Roger. "Hold those steps, will you?"

Once down and in the semidarkness, it was another matter. It was cold, and his memories of this place weren't good. He saw the rough stone face of the walls, where he had barked his knuckles—and looked at his hands, where the abrasions were healing. Not only he, but Francesca, had been imprisoned down here, if she were to be believed. He was inclined to think that she had told the truth; but he wanted evidence, wanted the sudden illuminating flash that would help him to see the whole truth.

"I'm coming," Mellish called, and climbed carefully down the steps. Their voices sounded holow. "Anything special you're looking for?"

"The odd chance. What was stored here, did you say?"

"Feeding-stuff for cattle. The cottage wasn't used for years, then this man Smith rented it, and lived here occasionally. They kept oil-cakes down here some winters, swedes, mangels, and turnips at other times."

Roger said: "Normal enough." He stood by the cemented patch in the wall. "I wonder why that's there. It doesn't seem to lead anywhere, it could hardly have been a window."

"Just a filled-in hole in the wall, I suppose," said Mellish.

"Could we have a look?"

Mellish was startled.

"Well—yes, I suppose so. It'll need some men on the job. You know what it's like breaking through a wall like that, and we can't use a pneumatic drill here. Well, we could, but it's hardly worth it. What do you expect to find?"

"I haven't the faintest idea. It just puzzles me."

Mellish sent for men and pickaxes. It was over an hour before they arrived, nearly an hour and a half before the cement was broken away, and the men were able to pull out pieces of the rock that made the walls of the cellar. It was nearly dark, and they were working in the light of smelly oil lamps and powerful electric torches. Mellish, unimpressed, was there with Roger; Burnaby was taking a breather upstairs.

A man exclaimed suddenly.

"Found something?" Mellish demanded, and stepped forward. His voice rose. "Great Scott!"

Roger, looking over his shoulder, saw the body of a man, doubled up in the hole in the wall.

22

COLD HOSPITALITY

The body was taken out of the hole carefully, laid on a tarpaulin, then lifted to ground level. There was little sign of putrefaction; the sealing up accounted for that. The light of car headlamps shone on the pale, slack face, the staring eyes, the nearly bald head, and the short gray beard. A bullet hole gaped in the right temple, and part of the back of the head was gone. The body was dressed in a light-brown suit, and Roger studied the cut of the clothes, and felt their smooth texture. The expensive-looking shoes were square-toed. The man wore a bow tie, quite as colorful as anything that Al Maloney had boasted.

"Do you know what I think?" Mellish asked in a strained voice.

"That he's an American?"

"That's right."

Roger said: "I think I can tell you his name, too. Al Maloney. Or that's a name he sometimes used." He went down on one knee, and felt inside the man's pocket. He found a billfold in the hip pocket, loose change in others, an American-made watch, a cigar-case, a book of matches with the words Hotel Algonquin on them. He opened the billfold and found some photographs, pound notes and dollar bills, and, printed in ink on the rough side of one of the sections, the name : A. Maloney.

There were three photographs : one of Francesca, identical with the one found in Kane's pocket, one of Mrs. Liddel, and one of a woman whom Roger had never seen.

"Found what you want?" asked Mellish.

"Not yet, but I think it will help," Roger said, "We'd better have him taken to London and do a post-mortem there. Can you fix it?"

"Of course. Er – West, I know what you're thinking. I ought to have been onto it at once." He was obviously distressed.

"No reason why you should," said Roger. "I was a long time getting round to it myself." He smiled, tautly. "I wonder if this will make Francesca Liddel talk."

* * * *

Francesca was in bed at the hospital, in a ground-floor ward very similar to the one in which Roger had been. She wore a fluffy pink bed jacket and pink pajamas. The rest had done her good, and she showed little sign of the physical ordeal from which she was recovering. The lack of makeup did not make her any less beautiful. She was leaning back on her pillows, reading a magazine, when she looked up to see Roger; she started.

"Hallo," said Roger. "Better?"

"Yes – thank you."

"Good. We had a lucky break, thanks apparently to Al Maloney. Did you know he got away and raised the alarm?"

"Did he?" She spoke flatly, wary and watchful again.

Roger pulled up a chair and sat opposite her, offering cigarettes; she took one, her fingers quite steady.

"He did. Al Maloney is proving quite a friend of yours, isn't he? Why did you go to America to see him?"

She didn't answer.

"I know that you did," said Roger. "I think you went because you discovered that a certain Al Maloney was blackmailing your father, and you went to try to make him stop. Lancelot Hay was party to the blackmail, but was sending the proceeds back to the States. Isn't that right?"

She drew deeply on the cigarette.

"And isn't it true that in the search, you found another, younger Al Maloney, a man very different in character from the man you were looking for?"

Francesca said in a strained voice: "How do you know all this?"

"Because I've found the original Al Maloney."

She started again: "*Here?* In England?"

"Yes."

"Has he told you—" She broke off.

"I'd rather you told me what it's about as far as you know. The rest will work itself out. The one certain thing is that the older Al Maloney will never be able to do any more harm."

There were tears in her eyes, making them shine; tears of relief. Her lips quivered for a moment, the cigarette nearly dropped. She took it out quickly, and leaned back with her eyes closed. Her breast rose and fell heavily under the strain of greater emotion than he could understand. It wasn't only relief.

She opened her eyes at last.

"Where did you find him?"

"It doesn't matter."

"All right," she said, "all right. I'll tell you what I can. Father *was* being blackmailed, and we discovered—"

"We?"

"Anthony and I. We discovered that it was being done through Lancelot, but that Lancelot was taking orders from this man Maloney. Maloney had been a friend of the family, years ago. Both of my mother and my father. He still wrote to Mother occasionally. I don't know how he discovered the truth—"

"What truth?"

"About my father's—other child."

Roger said: "Are you sure about that other child?"

"Of course I am. It was the only flaw in a perfect life. My father was—he *is* the most wonderful man I know. It was two years after their marriage—he was in Italy. He knew that if my mother discovered the truth, even after nearly thirty years, she would never understand or forgive.

You can't—explain—love. And he came to love Mother deeply. Anthony and I found out about it, because Lancelot used another man, you mentioned him the other day. Kane. Then Kane started to blackmail me. That is why I let him use the flat. I went to America to plead with Maloney, because the situation was beginning to affect my father's health. The demands for money were getting more and more insistent. He isn't wealthy, not really wealthy."

There was one flaw in this: it wasn't easy to send money to America in these days of currency control; was she telling the whole truth?

"I went to plead," Francesca went on. "Anthony stayed behind to look after Father."

"I thought they were on bad terms."

"That was because of Mother. She didn't approve of Anthony, they never got on. You must believe that."

"Yes, I can," said Roger.

"In America the first Maloney I found was—the man you know. Al." She closed her eyes again. "I knew he wasn't the man I'd gone to see, but he wouldn't leave me alone. He knew I was worried and wanted to help, but I wouldn't let him. I was still looking for the real Al Maloney when I heard about Lancelot's death and my father's arrest. I came straight home."

"I see," said Roger.

"I hadn't told Al about it, and didn't tell him why I had to leave. You see, I was—deeply in love with him."

Roger didn't speak.

"I was hardly in my right mind when I came back," Francesca went on. "The strain has been getting steadily worse for months; for nearly a year. Then I had this to face—father actually accused of murder. And I could believe that he *would* kill Lancelot. Even now, I don't know whether he did. If ever a man deserved killing, it was Lancelot. I was beside myself, torn both ways. I didn't want Al, *my* Al, to know. I ought to have realized that there was no way of keeping it from him. Do you remember how I behaved when that photographer took a picture of me?"

"I remember."

"I was beside myself and—I have always hated being

photographed, but that time it was to try to stop Al from seeing my photograph. Then I saw a chance of talking to a man who might know *your* side of the case — the editor. I offered the cameraman money, so that you couldn't guess I really wanted to talk to the editor. He was friendly. I didn't expect him to stop that photograph, but — well, he did. And he also confirmed what you'd made me believe — that Father was likely to be convicted."

Roger was nagged by a fear that she was keeping part, perhaps the vital part, to herself.

Roger said: "Miss Liddel, why did you tell me that your mother's life was in danger?"

She didn't answer.

"Whom did you suspect?"

She pressed her hand against her forehead and sat up.

"No one," she said.

"*What?*"

"No one," Francesca insisted. "I had to make you doubt whether Father was guilty. I thought that if you had reason to think someone else was in danger, you would begin to look for another suspect, that it would help my father. I didn't think my mother was in any danger at all."

Roger ruefully allowed that to sink in, and then began to smile. She was staring at him intently, and when the smile came, she relaxed, as if beginning to feel real relief.

"Not bad," congratulated Roger. "I fell for it completely. But the true word was spoken in jest. Your mother *has* been attacked."

She seemed appalled; incredulous.

* * * *

All through the case, Roger had thought that Francesca was withholding part of the truth; had doubted if she had lied directly as much as whether she had told him everything. He was sure that the news about the attack on Mrs. Liddel took her completely by surprise.

Slowly she whispered: "Was it — the other — Maloney?"

"We're not sure who it was."

"Is she — all right?"

"She'll recover."

"What—happened—to her?"

"She was poisoned—with arsenic."

"Oh, no," whispered Francesca. "No!" The significance of that, the probable truth that the killer of her cousin was still free, still alive, hit her very hard. And she wasn't really well enough to take these shocks.

"We still don't know the whole truth," Roger said. "Do you think your father killed Lancelot? Or do you think that your brother—"

"Tony," she said. "Tony?" She closed her eyes again. "But—but—why should he? Lancelot—he hated Lancelot, for what he was and what he had done. But Mother—why should anyone want to kill her? *Why?*"

"Perhaps because she knew the murderer."

"But she thought it was my father!"

"Are you sure?"

"Yes. Quite sure. She told you it was impossible, but when I went to see her she was bitter—hateful. Tony and I were there together. She blamed Father for everything, seemed to hate him for bringing this shame on her. She seemed so sure that it was he, she couldn't—" Francesca broke off.

Roger said gently: "What you're saying isn't evidence and can't be used against you or against anyone. Say exactly what you think. Let everything come."

"I've told you now," she said.

"Everything?"

"Everything that matters," she insisted. "You know why I went to see Kane, what hold he had over me. I've told you what happened at the cottage."

Her face was ghastly in its pallor and her body rigid; he marveled that she still kept her composure.

"You haven't told me two things," Roger said.

"What—are—they?"

"About the documents Kane came to find. Hadn't he asked for them before, hadn't he tried to make you give them up?"

"He'd talked to Tony, not to me. Tony didn't tell me what they were. I'm not even sure that he knew. I'd never heard of any documents, talk of them was a complete mystery to me."

It was easy to believe her, but it might be folly.

"What else do you want to know?" she asked.

"Why did you lie about not recognizing Kane at your flat when he came to see you?"

She raised her hands, helplessly.

"Yes, I did lie, it was Kane, and he wasn't disguised. He demanded the documents, and we said we hadn't got them. He went wild and hit Tony. I screamed, and he turned on me to keep me quiet. Soon after he began to search, the frontdoor bell rang. He pulled down his scarf and went out."

"Why not tell me this at the cottage?" asked Roger.

"I – I thought it would harm my father."

Roger now knew for certain that she had lied smoothly and plausibly before; she might be lying now.

"What about those documents Kane wanted?" he asked.

"I just don't know anything about them."

He didn't believe that.

"What about the sack he put over your head?"

"I – I invented that story," she said.

No wonder he didn't believe her!

"If this is everything, I still don't see why you didn't talk when I found you at the cottage. Why did you think you could do any good by keeping silent?"

"Isn't it obvious?" asked Francesca. "I was frightened. I *am* frightened. The old Maloney was still free. Fear of him has dictated nearly everything I've done for the past year. I was afraid of what he might do. I *am* afraid. I did exactly what he told me, through Kane; and he told me not to talk. I believe he was listening at the cottage and so – I didn't talk."

Roger said: "This man from London who questioned you. Wasn't it Maloney?"

"No."

"Did you recognize him?"

"I'd never seen him before, he was a complete stranger. He told me that he employed Kane. He knew everything that Kane and the old Maloney did, and I believed him. He was a short man, stocky, rather sallow. He didn't look English but his voice was English. I swear I've never seen him before."

"And he asked for these documents?"

"Yes."

Roger leaned forward.

"Miss Liddel, the life and death of your father, perhaps your brother, possibly Al Maloney and your mother, may depend on the truth being discovered soon. Be careful when you answer, remember what might happen if you lie. Do you know what documents these are?"

"No!" she cried.

"Do you think Tony does?"

"I don't think so, I'm not sure. He—"

She broke off, looking away. He was trying almost desperately to judge whether she was still lying when he saw the look of horror that froze her features. It was as sudden as a lightning flash.

He glanced round and saw the face at the window, saw a gun leveled at Francesca.

23

SHORT, DARK MAN

The threat had come swiftly, without warning—sudden menace with the shadow of death. Roger caught a glimpse of the man, jumped up, thrust out his hand and pushed Francesca back onto the pillows. He grabbed his chair and flung it with all his might. He saw the flash of flame and heard the roar of the shot. Then the chair crashed into the window.

The man disappeared.

Roger attempted to get out of the window, but pieces of glass were sticking out of the edges, and he couldn't move quickly enough; and the man out there would see him clearly against the light. He darted to one side, and called:

"Get under the bed. Get under the bed!"

Another shot roared, farther away; the bullet hit the wall above Francesca's head. Roger didn't see whether she was moving, didn't know whether she was hurt. He stretched out a hand to try to open the window; it was of the sash-cord type, but he couldn't get sufficient pressure on it. He swung round.

Francesca was falling onto her knees, at the side of the bed.

Someone came hurrying.

Roger opened the door, pushed past a nurse, and looked along the passage. A window at the far end was slightly open, and he could see the garden beyond. He reached the window and thrust it up. He heard another shot, and saw the flash, at least fifty yards away. He was still a good target, but there was a chance the gunman might not be looking toward him. He climbed out, dropping flat. Someone was shouting in alarm not far away, and there were other confused sounds. A passing motorist had the sense to switch on his headlights. They lit up the hospital grounds and showed a short man running toward the railings, which bordered a side street. The man had given up hope of killing Francesca, and was fleeing for his life.

Roger raced toward the railing. He was nearer a gate than was the man with the gun, and reached the pavement first. The motorist who had switched on his headlights had slowed down, and was almost at a standstill.

"What—" he began, out of the window.

"Police—get that man!"

The headlights bathed the man who had fired at the girl. He was climbing over the railings. He jumped down, turned away from the car, and began to run.

Roger jumped onto the running board.

"He's armed. Careful."

"Want me to—"

"Get after him." Roger clung to the door, as the car put on speed. Not far away from it he could see the man's legs, moving like pistons. He saw the man turn, and steeled himself for the shot. It missed. The car was now only a few yards behind the gunman, when he turned again and fired point blank at the driver.

Nothing happened.

"No ammo!" the driver shouted, and swung his wheel. "And look!"

Police were coming from the other end of the road.

The man with the gun hesitated, then doubled back, running in front of the car. It was slowing down, but couldn't stop quickly enough. Roger felt the impact. The man's face was grotesquely clear in the headlights, then disappeared into shadows below.

The wheels crunched over his body.

* * * *

The driver, shaken, stood by the side of the man, and muttered: "He's dead."

"It's what he asked for."

"He practically flung himself at me! I couldn't help it!"

"I know, don't worry. Go across to the hospital, will you, tell them what's happened, and ask them to bring a stretcher over here, right away. Then get yourself a drink."

The driver hurried off, a little unsteadily, and others drew up, among them a policeman. Roger said: "Look after things, Constable, and don't touch the body, don't let anyone else touch it. Except the stretcher-bearers from the hospital. Is that clear?"

"Yes, sir."

Roger took another look at the dead man's face. He had seen it at the window, for the man had made no attempt to hide. Round, sallow, with dark hair, broad features—an un-English face, which answered the description of Smith who had rented the cottage. There was no doubt about that.

Roger reached the hospital as the stretcher was brought out. The driver was with the orderlies.

"I'll support your statement to the constable," Roger said. "Tell him I'm West of the Yard."

He went in at the front entrance, forcing himself to an appearance of calm.

Francesca, back in bed, looked deathly pale, eyes like burning glass, but she was uninjured. Two nurses were with her, and one was holding a cup in front of her mouth.

She pushed it aside.

"The man from London?" Roger asked.

"Yes," she said, gaspingly. "Yes!"

"You needn't worry now," Roger said. "There's no more danger for you."

He hoped she would believe it, that he sounded as if it were true. He was sure that the man had tried to kill her to prevent her from talking; surely nothing could stop that now. Smith had believed that she could tell him what was in the mysterious documents.

He said: "Now let me have the whole truth, Miss Liddel."

She just stared at him, her mouth, her mind, closed to entreaty. He left her with the familiar, nagging disquiet more persistent than ever. He felt almost frightened, because he began to realize that he hadn't, as yet, even glimpsed the heart of the matter.

* * * *

Roger, telephoning Janet, told her nothing about the shooting. She had just returned from a theater, with Mark. The police were watching the house, and a neighbor had been sitter-in. Cheerfully, Roger replaced the receiver.

He spent half an hour with Mellish, stayed the night at The George and, with a full report on the dead man, the bullet from the old Maloney's head, and all papers from Smith's pockets in his own case, drove back to London early next morning. He was at the Yard soon after eleven o'clock. Twenty minutes later he knew that the bullet that had killed the elderly American had been fired from the gun Kane had used at Bell Street and at Hampstead.

Sloan told him there was no trace of Anthony Liddel.

"Begins to look as if he's one of our birds," Sloan said. "What happened at Stamford? Someone who didn't like you, or didn't like Francesca?"

"Both. I think she was to be silenced—and I'm beginning to believe that the shooting at Bell Street was for Maloney's benefit, not mine. The gunmen thought Francesca had told him everything."

"Had she?"

"I doubt if she knows everything. Is Coppell in?"

"I think so," said Sloan. "What's on your mind, Roger?"

Roger said: "A little bit of hell."

Coppell was not only in, but anxious to see him. He actually stood up when Roger entered, and shook hands.

Then he offered cigarettes, and said gruffly that he wasn't able to approve of anyone being shot at so often.

Roger forced a smile. "It's time I took young Maloney's advice, I think."

"About what?"

"Carrying a gun."

"If you want one, get a permit," said Coppell. "But didn't you get the man who fired at Miss Liddel?"

"He got himself." Roger related what had happened, and began to lay the things taken from the dead man's pockets on Coppell's table. He didn't try to anticipate Coppell's reaction. "There isn't much more, sir—identity card in the name of Smith and, I think, a forged one. Oddments such as stamps, a penknife, cheap watch—nothing which really helps us to find out much about him. I telephoned particulars last night, and his fingerprints will be here by now, we'll soon know whether he has a record."

"No farther ahead?" It was almost a complaint.

"I think we now know the real situation where Francesca Liddel and her Al Maloney are concerned. I wouldn't like to claim more. The case is turning on the nature of the documents and the identity of the people who want them. Kane was only an agent. Maloney—the dead Maloney—was probably one also. Lancelot Hay started on his own as a nasty piece of work, before he, too, followed suit. When the pressure really hotted up, and Liddel was being pressed to give up these mysterious documents, Hay was killed. There was no violence while he was dealing with money, but once the documents came into it, killing started."

Coppell's heavy, dark eyebrows seemed to meet.

"Meaning?"

"Just what I say, sir—the documents now prove to be the crucial factor. Where are they, what are they, and who wants them? We could believe that Anthony Liddel, say, would risk a lot to save himself from being caught and hanged, but this Mr. Smith got himself killed. It almost looked as if he meant to make sure that he couldn't be properly identified. I think he took the case out of its present level to a much higher one. Or lower."

Coppell grunted.

Roger said formally: "We've felt that there was something odd about this case from the beginning. Some of the people concerned are prepared to kill rather than be caught and questioned. They've plenty of money—they were able to buy the allegiance of the farmer and his son up north; able to buy Kane's allegiance; able to make Lancelot Hay do what they wanted. They want certain documents, and will do murder to make sure that no one who might know the secret of the documents can explain them to us. That is all clear, isn't it?"

"Perfectly."

"Four questions need answering." Roger was brisk, almost abrupt. "Where are the papers? Who has the papers? What are they? Who wants them? And I think we could safely guess at the last answer now."

"Although you don't like guessing," said Coppell, almost sourly.

"Sometimes it's necessary."

"Well, guess."

Roger shrugged. "Agents of a foreign power. Spies." He gave a short laugh. "It's time we consulted the Special Branch about this—and time we took another look at James Liddel's history. Until recently, he was a highly placed civil servant, working at the Foreign Office. I've had that fact at the back of my mind all the time. We need to find out what documents he had access to before he retired; whether there's any leakage from the department he controlled. Not my job, sir, but the quicker we can get the information, the better."

Coppell frowned.

"I'll go over to the F.O. myself. Want to come?"

"I'd rather stick to my own end of it."

"Seeing James Liddel again?"

"That can come when we know the answer from the Foreign Office. There's Anthony Liddel's part to find out, and the motive for the attack on his mother."

"Assuming that he poisoned her?"

"That someone did—presumably, just because she knows or might know the truth about these documents. Sloan tells me we're not allowed to question her yet. Her own doctor will postpone questioning as long as he can.

This might not stand delay, we have to find those documents."

"Ah," said Coppell. "I wondered when you were coming to that. Think Anthony Liddel has them?"

Roger shrugged.

* * * *

He went across to Cannon Row where Kane was still held, but the man resisted all attempts to make him talk, although he showed signs of nervousness. The spell in jail hadn't yet had any effect on the man's nerves, but the wearing process was only beginning.

Roger put his hand to his pocket and drew out a photograph, face downward. Kane's gaze fell toward it, then lifted again, immediately. Roger kept the picture face downward.

"We know you were being employed by someone," he said. "If you want to save your neck, you'd better tell us who it was."

"You can't fix me," Kane sneered.

"Think not? You'll change your mind when you know what we've found in Smith's cottage. Why did you kill Maloney?"

Kane started violently.

"Beginning to see? Why kill a bald-headed American on a lonely English farm?"

Now Kane was really shaken.

"You—you can't fix that on me."

Roger turned the photograph over; it was of the old Maloney, taken after death.

"Recognize him?" he demanded roughly.

Kane stared at it, as if hypnotized, and his lips began to work. He gave a curious little sound, and then rubbed his hands together raspingly. It made the quiet of the police station seem more intense. Kane's eyes never wavered from the picture, which showed horrifyingly how he had died.

Roger said: "The bullet in his head was fired from the gun you used when you fired at me, Kane."

"I didn't kill him!"

"Then who did?"

"I—"

Roger said: "Ever seen him before?" and flashed a photograph of the dead Smith out of his pocket. Kane caught sight of it, blanched, and jumped to his feet. His nerves couldn't hold out any longer, and he began to tremble violently, his teeth chattering.

"He must have killed Maloney! He was at the cottage, he met Maloney there alone, I was in London. I can prove I was in London. Smith must have killed him. He gave me the gun afterwards!"

"Smith?" Roger barked.

"That man."

"He doesn't look like a Smith. Who is he?"

Kane almost screamed: "I don't know! But he brought me into it, I wouldn't have touched it if he hadn't. He must have killed Maloney. I tell you I didn't know Maloney was dead!"

"Tell me what documents you were after!"

"I don't know!" cried Kane, but his eyes said that he was lying.

"So you still pretend you don't know what was in them?"

"I didn't kill Maloney and—but *look!* Smith's dead—that's a dead man's face." He clutched his throat. *"Who killed him?"*

Roger said: "His employers don't take much account of a life here and there. They sacrificed him and Maloney. They'll sacrifice you and anyone else to suit themselves. Who was Smith working for, Kane?"

"I tell you I don't know!" Kane shouted the words, then swung round, staggered to the bed in the corner, and dropped down on it, his hands in front of his face. His nerve had broken as suddenly as a cut string. "He brought me into it, he staked me, he let me have everything I could make on the side. But I didn't kill anyone."

Roger wasn't satisfied, but doubted whether Kane could tell him any more. He was certain that Smith had employers, and that the truth was only just beginning to show. If Kane could tell more, he would have; there was no resistance left in him.

There remained Anthony Liddel—and young Al Maloney. Was it a mistake to believe that Francesca's Al was completely innocent? On the evidence, no one could assume it with any certainty. There might still be a thick façade of lies and intrigue to pull down.

He walked across the Yard toward the Civil Police building, and when he was going through the passages, Eddie Day called out:

"Handsome!"

"Hallo, Eddie."

"The A.C. wants to see you. Quick."

"Thanks," said Roger. Without noticeably hurrying he was at the Assistant Commissioner's office in less than five minutes. He tapped and went in. His mind, full of Kane and the man's complete collapse, leaped forward in expectation at Coppell's glowering expression.

Roger caught his breath.

What was missing from Liddel's old department?

"You wanted to see me, sir."

"Handsome, are you sure you've got this job right?"

"I think so."

"I'm not so sure. I've been talking to the Permanent Secretary at the Foreign Office. I don't like being laughed at. Liddel left everything in perfect order. Nothing at all is missing."

24

THE LOVERS

"What-ho, Handsome," said Eddie Day genially. "Still got the same bee in your bonnet? You've been going around for a week with a face as long as a month of Sundays. You want to cheer up—Liddel's not the only fish in the sea."

"Too true," said Roger. "I'll see you, Eddie."

Eddie, who had met him outside his office, looked more like a predatory fish than ever.

Sloan was in the office.

"You're earlier than I expected," he said, as Roger went to his desk.

It was not, in fact, seven days since Coppell had been so decisively reassured by the Foreign Office; it was five. Liddel had been up for a second hearing, and remanded again for eight days, after formal evidence; the hearing had been over in forty minutes. Anthony Liddel was still missing. Kane had signed a statement admitting that he had received orders from Smith, but declaring that he did not know for whom Smith worked. A verdict of murder against some person or persons unknown had been returned at the inquest on Aloysius Conway Maloney of New York City — and the American consular official who had held a watching brief had made no comment. There was no further identification of Smith; it had been discovered that he lived in a Kensington boarding house, had been there for nearly two years, and as far as his landlady had known, he was a commercial traveler. He had always been a most secretive man. Except that the place where he sometimes ate had been found, there was no other information. A formal verdict of suicide had been returned at the Stamford inquest on him. The press had been there in force, but had been disappointed of sensation.

Francesca was back in London, at her flat.

Young Al Maloney was still at her brother's flat.

Mrs. Liddel had almost recovered. Neither she nor her husband had made any further statement. She had not admitted that her son had visited her on the morning that she had been found ill. No trace of arsenic was found in her room, but she had undoubtedly taken arsenic and, but for the prompt attention, she would probably have died.

James Liddel retained his almost unnatural composure; since the shock he had received at mention of the name Maloney, he had given no sign that Roger had found helpful.

According to Kane, he had seen Lancelot Hay several times, and Hay had shown great cunning in blackmailing his uncle. Kane obviously believed that Liddel had murdered his nephew; and there was still no definite evidence against that. On the other hand, Gabriel Potter and the counsel he briefed would undoubtedly use the illness of Mrs. Liddel as a pointer to the probability that the real murderer was still at large.

Neither of the Shepton Harrings had been found, but it was now evident that they had let the cottage to Smith, and had done what they had been told, saying nothing and accepting payment.

"You're letting this get on your mind too much," Sloan protested. "Liddel will probably be found not guilty, and as you doubt whether he killed the man, what's your quarrel with that? We're bound to find Anthony Liddel before long."

Roger shrugged.

"Bill, I still don't believe the simple blackmail story, but I can't see beyond it since the Foreign Office fiasco. Smith, Kane, and the Harrings weren't really interested in Liddel's sullied past. They wanted a hold on him, and they wanted these documents. We're still stuck. I don't like it, because there might be a lot that we don't know. I suppose the Foreign Office could have been fooled."

Sloan made no comment.

"You don't believe it, no one believes it," Roger said. "You think this story of the documents was a red herring, that we struck a blackmailing gang, and they died out with Smith—unless Anthony Liddel was involved, in which case it will die out with him. Nice and tidy, but not true."

"I've never known you wrong, but also I've never known you so obstinate," Sloan said slowly. "There isn't even a real dead end, except Liddel—no inquiries are outstanding."

"Except one."

"What's that?"

"We've never had an answer from New York about our murdered Maloney."

"That means they've no useful information," said Sloan.

"The next step," said Roger, "is to advise me to take a holiday. Coppell was on the point of it. Any news of Francesca and her Al today?"

"Yes," said Sloan, and smiled faintly. "They spent the morning at the zoo, had lunch at Les Gourmets in Greek Street, and went to Hillcourt Mews at about three o'clock. They've spent practically every minute together since she got back. Why they don't get married, I can't understand."

"Delicacy—they've got to wait until the verdict," said Roger. "I think I'll look them up."
Sloan didn't speak.
The telephone rang.
"Yes, what is it?" Sloan asked. Roger glanced through some reports on his desk, none of them to do with the Liddel case. As always at a time of stress his desk was scrupulously neat. He noticed the change in Sloan's tone, and looked up. "Yes, send it along right away," Sloan said. "As soon as it's decoded."
He put the receiver down.
"Well?" asked Roger.
"There's a long cable in from New York. In code. It contains the name Maloney," said Sloan.

* * * *

Roger felt his nerves tingling as he took the decoded cable. Sloan leaned over his shoulder. The clerk who had brought it in closed the door with a snap. Roger began to read, and Sloan exclaimed: "Well, well!" They read on:

Highly confidential report on Aloysius Conway Maloney. Aged sixty-one American citizen British origin suspected espionage 1943–1945 interned released September 1945 out of country nine months watched on return known to associate with unfriendly aliens interrogated prior Alger Hiss trial released due lack of evidence closely watched Federal Bureau Investigation known associates British and other aliens remained suspected espionage left New York five weeks ago destination supposed Texas no further trace this side reported found dead England advise close check identity marks two inch dark brown mole right breast, little finger left hand three-eighths inch shorter than right hand fingerprints being radioed request comparison and confirmation identify earliest

"So you weren't wrong," Sloan said. "I wonder what Coppell will say when he sees this little lot."
"Sit on them, will you? Compare them with the general

description as soon as you can, and if I'm not back, telephone me at Hillcourt Mews."

"So you're going there?"

"I'm just in the mood to discuss matters with a man named Maloney," said Roger. "I wish I could be sure whether the live Maloney really is an orphan."

* * * *

Al Maloney opened the door wide, and gave a mock bow. He looked fit and buoyant. He was dressed in a dark-gray suit, and his tie obviously hadn't been bought in the Tie Shop on Broadway. His blond hair was brushed as flat as it would go, fining down his features to an almost aggressive angularity, but there was still that indefinable, likeable quality about him as he ushered Roger into the big living room.

Francesca was sitting in an armchair.

"Look what the good Lord's sent us," said Maloney. "Sit down, Superintendent."

Whatever secret worries Francesca might have, she hid them well. She looked lovelier than Roger had ever seen her. She held out her hand; it was cool and firm. He stood back, and studied her.

"Yes, I'm a lucky man," Maloney said. "You couldn't be more welcome, Superintendent. We wanted to tell the world, and you'll do for a start. Isn't that so, Frankie?"

"Meaning what?" asked Roger.

"My gay bachelor days are over," said Maloney, "and that goes for Frankie's too. There ought to be champagne!"

"What inspired this?" asked Roger drily. "The birds of paradise or the chimpanzees?"

Maloney roared.

"You're good! I'll tell you, West, it was in the aquarium. Frankie agrees with me, though, your zoo can't compare with Central Park for romance."

"Do you have to have us watched wherever we go?" asked Francesca. "Aren't you, even now, satisfied with what we've told you?"

"And if I were, I'd still keep you under surveillance."

"I suppose you think that Tony will get in touch with us," Francesca said. She was serious, but did not give the impression that she was worried. "I don't think he will, he'll be afraid that you'll be watching all the time. Are you going through with my father's trial?"

"Your father and your brother could have conspired together."

Francesca said: "The trouble is that you don't really know them. I don't think either of them killed Lancelot, and I don't believe that Tony tried to kill my mother. He might kill in a fit of rage, but he would never use poison. Poison isn't a weapon my father would use, either. Don't you take things like that into consideration?"

"Certainly we do, and weigh them up against the fact that arsenic was used and your father bought some," Roger said.

"Do we have to go on with this?" asked Maloney. "Frankie's tired of it, and so am I."

"Are you sure you've never met the older Maloney?"

"I'm sure," said Maloney. "I owe that guy one big debt, and I wish I could pay it. If Frankie hadn't gone to New York looking for him, she would never have met me." His good spirits seemed irrepressible. "Frankie agrees with me, it's almost worth what happened to her at that cottage."

Roger said: "I doubt it. Miss Liddel—"

"Oh, forget it," Maloney said.

"Miss Liddel, I'm sorry to harp on a distasteful matter, but you knew, didn't you, that your father was blackmailed because of a son born out of wedlock?"

"She told you about it," said Maloney.

"Of course," Francesca said.

"Have you ever heard what happened to this son?"

"No."

"Do you know how old he'd be?"

"Twenty-eight."

"Did you ever discuss what happened to him, with your father?"

"Only briefly."

"When was that?"

"After I had discovered about the blackmail. My father told me the story then. The child was adopted—he did not

160

tell me by whom. He paid the foster parents well, a lump sum, and has never heard from them since. What *are* you thinking about now?"

"Coincidences," said Roger. "Are you sure you haven't heard from your brother since he disappeared?"

"I am quite sure."

"You've no idea where he is?"

Maloney intervened in a quiet voice.

"West, we've agreed it's possible that Tony killed himself. We think that maybe he killed Lancelot and is afraid of it being proved against him."

"I doubt that theory," Roger said.

"Why?" Francesca's voice was sharp. "Have you heard more about him?"

"Not yet. But if he killed himself, he wouldn't do it so that no one could find his body. Murderers sometimes hide bodies for a while, suicides don't find it so easy. Bodies always turn up, Miss Liddel. And if he killed himself, it would be as a confession—his death would practically prove his father's innocence. Did he have any friends you haven't told us about?"

"No."

"There's a time to stop guessing," Maloney said. "That's mostly all you've done. You only guess about James Liddel. You only guess about Tony visiting his mother and poisoning her."

The telephone rang, and Maloney moved across the room and picked it up. He looked at Francesca, and his eyes glowed; as if he worshiped her. Probably he did. That coincidence still rankled in Roger's mind; fear, for these two, and for much else.

"Yeah?" said Maloney, into the telephone, and then added: "Sure, he's right here. For you, West."

"Thanks."

It was Sloan.

"Take it easy, Roger," Sloan said, an obvious warning that big news was coming. "We've had the old Maloney's prints in. They're the same as the dead man's. No doubt about his identity—he was the suspected spy."

Roger said casually: "I see, go on."

"Then we've had a message from Nurse James—you

remember, the nurse we had with Mrs. Liddel. She was taken off that duty yesterday, as arranged."

"Yes?" Roger knew that Francesca and Maloney were watching him closely. Maloney moved across the room and rested a hand on Francesca's shoulder. They made a fine couple. Damn fine couple!

"She says she'd been teased by something at Maybury Crescent all the time, and couldn't think what it was, so couldn't report it. Now she thinks she's seen a glimmering. There was a visitor on the morning of the arsenic poisoning —a man. Maisie denied seeing anyone, but let the truth out the same evening. Nurse James took it in, but didn't spot the significance at the time. The phrase was 'He'll be back,' when she was talking to the cook. A young man with fair hair called at the back door that morning, according to a window cleaner who was working at a house opposite. Nurse James remembered this window cleaner, saw him in the district again, and spoke to him. Anthony Liddel had been there all right, and Maisie the maid lied."

Roger was looking blankly out of the window, hoping that he wasn't showing his excitement.

"That means Maisie and the cook were prepared to lie about Anthony's visit—he had them where he wanted them," Sloan went on. "You might get plenty out of them if you have a go."

"That's all?"

"Isn't it enough?"

Roger smiled faintly: he wanted to grin like a Cheshire cat.

"Not quite. I'll be seeing you, Bill."

He rang off. The others still watched him closely. He ran his fingers through his hair, and took out cigarettes, thinking: Maisie said, "He'll be back." It's the last place I thought of looking, but Tony's at Maybury Crescent or I'm a Dutchman. The servants are hiding him.

"You're looking smug," Maloney said. "Guessing again?"

Roger said: "I guess so," laughed, and went out.

25

TOP FLOOR

Roger pulled up alongside a telephone kiosk, round the corner, and telephoned Sloan again.

"I'll be with you in twenty minutes," he said. "Meanwhile, have the watch on 11 Maybury Crescent doubled, back and front. It must be unobtrusive."

"Right."

"I'll want a word with Nurse James as soon as I get in," Roger said, and rang off.

He sat at the wheel, watching the passing traffic, picturing the house at Maybury Crescent and the timid, flat-chested Maisie. He laughed suddenly, and a man stared at him as he let in the clutch and drove off.

Sloan and Nurse James were in his office. In plain clothes the woman looked attractive in a severe way; she was anxious and apologetic.

"I'm extremely sorry, sir, but I just didn't realize whom Maisie might mean when she said that to the cook. It wasn't until I left the house and was thinking it over that the significance struck me. There's no doubt she used the words 'He'll be back' — and it almost certainly referred to Anthony Liddel. Maisie was very fond of him — so was the cook. I'm so annoyed with myself."

"You've done a lot better than you realize," Roger said briskly. "Make a detailed statement, covering everything that you noticed and overheard at the house. Have it ready first thing tomorrow morning, will you?"

"Yes, sir, of course."

Sloan, who had sat at the desk throughout this exchange, stifled a yawn.

"Tired?" Roger seemed to be bursting with vitality.

"I've been sitting here too long — I've hardly moved since I came back," said Sloan.

"You're going to do something tonight. I wouldn't take anyone else on this job if I were paid for it. I'd like Burnaby, too."

"What's brewing?"

"A raid on the Liddels' house, after dark. I've still got Maisie's back-door key. If they have no warning, they won't be able to cover up, and I fancy we'll find Anthony living a life of luxury."

"You'll want a search warrant."

"Coppell won't argue about that." Roger picked up the cable from New York, and the Yard pictures of the elder Maloney's fingerprints. Next he took out a piece of plain paper, and printed several words carefully. Sloan didn't notice what he was doing. He put the note in a plain envelope, sealed it, and printed the name and address. Then he rang for a messenger.

"Have that delivered to 11 Maybury Crescent at once," he said.

Sloan looked up. "Now what?"

"Just an anonymous letter," Roger said airily, "in the right tradition. It was that way this case started."

* * * *

The night was perfect for the raid. A steady wind blew, there was a drizzle of rain, and heavy clouds hid the stars. The lamp lighting in Maybury Crescent wasn't good. Roger stopped his car at the end of the street. Burnaby and Sloan went round to the back of the house, while Roger had a word with one of the two men on duty.

"Anyone gone in or come out?" Roger asked.

"Two ladies called about six o'clock, and stayed for three-quarters of an hour — they've called before. Friends of Mrs. Liddel, I believe, sir." The watching detective was very precise.

"Anyone else?"

"Nothing seen from here, sir."

"Thanks. I'll be going in at the back. We've more men at each end of the street. If anyone comes out in a hurry, don't take unnecessary chances. He might be armed."

"Right, sir."

Roger joined Sloan, who had been talking to the men on duty. The cook had been out for twenty minutes or so, but was back. Maisie hadn't left the house during the day. The light was now on in the maids' parlor; it was after eight-thirty, probably they had finished work for the night. The parlor, Roger knew, led off the kitchen; it was possible to get in without being noticed—and to go to the main part of the house.

"Warned them what might happen?" Roger asked.

"All set," said Sloan.

"Good. Burnaby, let's go."

The three men walked to the back entrance of Number 11. The parlor light showed at the sides and the top of the curtains; no other light was visible.

Roger reached the back door first, and took out Maisie's key. He could hear nothing except the bated breathing of his men. He inserted the key, twisted, and pushed. The door opened without a sound.

It was darker inside than out.

Roger went in, cautiously. There was nothing in his way. He waited until his eyes were accustomed to the gloom, then opened the door that led to the front of the house. Just to the left there was light coming from beneath a door—that of the maids' parlor. This light was sufficient to show them the furniture in the kitchen, and the passage that led to the front hall. Another dim light was on, probably on the first-floor landing.

Roger found the handle of the parlor door.

He thrust the door open.

Maisie was sitting at one side of the fireplace. The cook, a bigger woman but just as flat-chested, had her back to the door. Maisie gave a stifled shriek, and jumped up, dropping a stocking she was mending. The cook jerked her head round.

"Just keep quiet," Roger said. He slipped into the room and Sloan followed him. Burnaby closed the door and stood on guard outside. Neither of the women spoke, but stared at the two detectives, Maisie's mouth opening and shutting, the cook's tightly closed.

"Well, Maisie," Roger said heavily, "who told you to lie to the police?"

Maisie raised her hands.

"You've no right—"

"I've every right. Is Mr. Anthony upstairs now?"

Maisie didn't answer, but dropped into her chair and began to tremble violently. The cook muttered under her breath. Then Maisie began to cry. Sobs wracked her body. She covered her face with her hands, and didn't look up.

"Yes he is," the cook said tremulously. "On the top floor."

* * * *

Roger told them authoritatively to put on their outdoor clothes, and sent them, with Burnaby, to the nearest police car. After a few hours waiting at Scotland Yard they would probably be ready to talk. The cook kept a sullen silence, and Maisie was crying quietly.

Burnaby came back while Roger and Sloan were still downstairs.

"All okay, sir!"

"All right, here we go," said Roger. "We'll listen outside Mrs. Liddel's door. If there's no one talking, you'll stay on guard there, and we'll go up."

"Yes, sir." Burnaby swallowed his disappointment.

Roger stopped at the half-landing and opened the door of the darkroom. He switched on the light; everything was as he had last seen it. Mrs. Liddel had not taken up her hobby again.

He sensed the others' impatience.

"We're not due until nine o'clock," he said.

Neither of the others spoke.

Roger led the way upstairs, tense, expectant. The landing light was on, and showed all the doors, including that of Mrs. Liddel's room. No light glowed at the edges of that door. They stood outside it, but heard nothing.

"Asleep, probably," Burnaby said.

"Stay here, and be careful," Roger said.

With Sloan, he looked in each of the bedrooms; they were empty. Liddel's small library had a stale smell, as if the door hadn't been opened for weeks. That done, they went to the foot of the second flight of stairs, leading to the top floor and the maids' quarters. These stairs were carpeted, but they creaked. Roger walked up by the wall to lessen the squeaking. They reached another landing, and saw a light beneath a door that was immediately opposite.

"Think he has it locked?" Sloan whispered.

"Could have." Roger approached cautiously, and turned the handle. Before he tried to thrust the door open, he heard a voice, a woman's voice.

"*Yes, I know,*" she said.

Roger didn't recognize her voice, nor had he reckoned on Anthony Liddel having company.

"*I've known all the time,*" the woman went on. Her voice was pitched so low that it lost all its identity; it was just a voice, and there was only one emotion in it – deadly malice. Even through the closed door, that sounded clearly.

"*All the time,*" she repeated.

A man exclaimed: "*You devil!*"

"Words won't help you," the woman said. "*Tell me where those papers are, Tony.*"

So the man *was* Anthony Liddel.

"*Tell me where they are,*" the woman said, "*or it will be the worse for you.*" The simple words increased that feeling of deadliness. Here was a woman who knew exactly what she wanted, and who was threatening; and a man who was frightened. They could sense that.

"*I – I don't know!*" Liddel said at last. "*Get away. Put that gun down.*"

"No," the woman said. "*If you don't tell me at once, I shall shoot you where it will be very painful.*" She laughed; the laugh had an edge to it. "*I am not playing. Be quick.*"

Roger took his gun out of his pocket, held the handle of the door with the fingers of his left hand, turned again – and thrust the door open. The bright light dazzled him, but he saw the woman swing round, and saw the gun in her hand.

"Look out!" Sloan shouted.

Roger swayed to one side as the woman fired. It was Mrs. Liddel, in a dressing gown, tall, regal; she would have been lovely, but for the distorted twist of her face, the venom in her eyes. The shot roared out, and the bullet thudded into the wall.

Anthony Liddel jumped forward and clutched at her arm. She kicked at him, but he didn't let go. Roger, moving swiftly, gripped her wrist. The gun fell heavily. As it fell, Liddel released his mother, and she turned on Roger like a wildcat, clawing, kicking, glaring.

26

THE DOCUMENTS

Sloan gripped the frenzied woman round the waist, and pulled her away from Roger, still struggling. Sloan dragged her to a chair and pulled her into it, then held her shoulders tightly. She was gasping for breath, her face distorted, her eyes glittered as if they were the eyes of a fiend. She made a rattling noise in her throat; mouthing gibberish.

Tony Liddel stood by the bed, his face pale and haunted. He sat down, heavily.

Roger shrugged his coat into position. The woman had scratched his right cheek; he dabbed at it with his handkerchief. Without speaking, he noted the woman's still uncontrollable frenzy, and, taking a pair of handcuffs from his pocket, fastened one round her wrist and the other round the wooden arm of the chair. They clicked. He drew back, as she glared up at him.

Then a bell rang downstairs.

Sloan said tensely: "Who's that?"

"Tell Burnaby to find out."

Sloan nodded, and went off, leaving the door open. Tony Liddel sat up, wearily, the shadows still in his eyes.

Roger said: "Bad time, Mr. Liddel?"

"Bad!" Liddel groped for cigarettes with trembling fingers.

Roger flicked his lighter; the cigarette shook so much that the end put the flame out. Roger flicked again.

Tony drew in the smoke. "Thanks."

The woman was staring now, but making no sound.

"When did you know for certain that it was your mother?" Roger asked.

"Not until—ten minutes ago. When she came here. I'd been afraid—we were all afraid—" He broke off.

"Sure you didn't find out some time ago, and try to kill her, because of it?"

"I didn't try to kill her!"

"Why did you run away?"

Liddel said: "I thought it might help Father, bring suspicion on me. That's why I lied about not going to see Mother, and I made Maisie promise not to tell. Call me a hero!" He gave a nervous little laugh. "You see, I knew—"

He broke off.

Roger said evenly: "You knew that your mother photographed documents of great importance which your father brought home, and sold or gave the photostats away, didn't you?"

Liddel muttered: "Yes – yes. I was a long time getting round to it, but—"

He broke off.

Roger heard Sloan coming back, and voices downstairs; they seemed a long way off.

"Hallo, Bill. Know who it is?" Roger asked.

"Maloney and Francesca, I think."

"Let them come up," Roger said.

Sloan went to the landing and called down.

Maloney came in first, Francesca wasn't far behind him. They saw Mrs. Liddel, handcuffed, and Francesca stopped; then her gaze swept round the room. Slowly, she went forward, toward her mother. As she drew within reach, Mrs. Liddel struck at her with her free hand.

"What—what has happened?" Francesca's voice was barely audible, and Maloney stood speechless for once.

"We know what it's all about, now," said Roger. "We know who killed Lancelot Hay, and that your father was prepared to take the blame for it, because he didn't know the whole truth. You suspected that truth."

Francesca said wearily, but evasively: "How can you be sure it was Mother?"

"Oh, she did it," Tony said. "She told me she did it. Boasted of it. She asked Father to buy the arsenic for her, for weed killing. She'd known Lancelot was blackmailing Father, and relished it. She'd been selling State secrets for years, photographing papers Father brought home. That wonderful hobby of hers! She only needed a few minutes for each job, then passed them on to Lancelot."

Francesca closed her eyes; her mother glared at Liddel like a wild thing.

"Lancelot blackmailed Father about the illegitimate child, too — playing them off against each other. When Father retired, there were no more documents, and Lancelot started to blackmail Mother — about her spying.

"So she decided to kill him — and had the hellish idea of framing Father for it. She knew Lancelot was blackmailing Father, guessed where he was going that night, and told Lancelot she had to see him before dinner. They had drinks, and she slipped arsenic into Lancelot's glass.

"Father knew she'd killed Lancelot, knew she knew about the other child, and — being Father! — was prepared to hang to save her. He'd call it an act of atonement. Lancelot had been blackmailing him for years, of course — but I can't guess what reason he thought Mother had for killing Lancelot."

"Can you?" Roger asked Francesca.

She shook her head.

Tony went on: "She thought there would be no more trouble after Lancelot was dead, but Smith put pressure on her to get those last documents. He threatened her with exposure, and she tried desperately to get them. She was terrified by the man, he had her where he wanted her."

Maloney said: "Hell!" He turned to Roger. "Call me a fool, West, but I knew a bit about this. Frankie told me, and I wanted to help. No more harm could be done with State papers, as her father had resigned, and — no one could be sure. They just had to be sure."

"That's right," Liddel said heavily. "We didn't want to believe it. We thought the obvious thing might be true, that she hated Father because of the other son. Father believed it was why she did it, and wouldn't say a word to help himself. He called it making amends for that other son."

"It must have turned her mind," Francesca said, poignantly.

Her mother had fallen, now, into a stupor, her eyes half-closed.

Roger said: "Why did she kill Lancelot?"

"He began to blackmail her, as I told you, after Father retired, and there were no more documents. He was only a go-between, and didn't get much out of it. Mother let it all out, before you came. She'd started years ago, working with an old family friend — Al Maloney. He was an agent for a foreign power. She had some dealings with a man named Smith, a big-shot agent in England, too. Have you caught up with Smith?" He looked at Roger.

"Yes," said Roger. "What we don't know yet is who told you about that cottage near Stamford, and who sent those anonymous letters to the Yard."

Liddel said: "Well, I can answer that one. Maisie."

"*What?*" cried Roger.

"Poor, dumb, timid Maisie. She hated Mother, because she was once engaged to a chauffeur here, who stole a few pounds. The chauffeur went to prison, and died while there. Maisie blamed Mother for his death. She guessed Mother had killed Lancelot, and sent those letters — she hadn't the courage to name her. It all misfired. Then — "

"But the message about the cottage? How did she know that?"

"She was in Smith's pay. She knew Kane, and was a good go-between up to a point, but her hatred of Mother made her send those anonymous letters. When Maisie saw how it was going she tried to poison Mother."

"How do you know?" Roger demanded sharply.

"Maisie told me," Liddel said. "She's always had a soft spot for me. She let me hide here, and I was waiting for a chance to get the whole truth, just to save my father." He paused. "I thought I had a chance to, tonight. It's a special brand of hell to see your own mother as an inhuman devil, but I'd come round to it. Everything Frankie and I had feared was true. Frankie went to the States, to see the older Maloney, and to find out if there really was something more in it than an illegitimate son. She'd learned a little, and — well, we were desperate, even before Lancelot was killed."

"What made you desperate so early?"

"It really started when Kane put the squeeze on us. Before she left for the States, Frankie found some photostats in Mother's room and a letter to Maloney. She knew then what Mother had done, but didn't know why. Was she being blackmailed, or—" Liddel broke off. "We just had to discover if the same kind of thing had happened before.

"Frankie didn't find the real Maloney, though. He had been recalled to England. He telephoned my mother over here, and said he was in some trouble."

"I see," said Roger. "He was in trouble, all right, his employers had sentenced him to death. Liddel, can you tell me what particular documents Kane was so anxious to get?"

Francesca said: "The photographs I saw in Mother's room. They were stolen, and Kane thought one of us had taken them. We lied because of them, wanting to save Father, but didn't want to let anyone know about Mother and the documents. I nearly failed when I blurted out something about the documents Kane wanted from Tony."

Maloney drew her close to him.

"All I knew, honey, was that Kane was giving you hell. I could have killed him, and came close to doing it. West thought I was in the plot. Who can blame him?"

"Have you the photostats?" Roger asked Francesca.

"No."

"No," echoed Liddel.

* * * *

"There's one angle we haven't tried, yet," Roger said to Sloan.

"I can guess which. Roger, what was that anonymous letter you talked about?"

Roger laughed.

"A note to Mrs. Liddel, telling her that her son was likely to visit her. I wanted her worked up about that. Forget it, and tell me why Mrs. Liddel ever got into it, and why she hated her husband so much."

"Don't ask me," said Sloan.

* * * *

James Liddel was in bed, but the light was on in his cell, and he was reading; as Roger drew near, he saw that the book was Gibbon's *Decline and Fall.* Liddel smiled and put the book on the small chair at the bedside. His face was lined and worn, but his calm remained. He waved toward the foot of the bed.

"Please sit down, Mr. West."

"Thanks."

"You must find your duties onerous, if they keep you busy so late as this."

"They are very onerous," said Roger. "Mr. Liddel, what did you do with the photographs of the last set of documents which your wife obtained?"

The effect of the question was as great as the effect of the name Maloney had been. Liddel's composure was wiped away. In a single second he seemed to become older, all his defenses crumbling.

Roger said quietly: "You see, we know that Mrs. Liddel killed your nephew, and that you realized it. We know that you preferred to suffer for it, because of a sense of loyalty —a very great sense of loyalty, and everyone must admire you for it. We know that she discovered about your other son with the help of a private inquiry agent, and made you think that explained her actions. We know that she was dealing with enemy agents for years. The one thing we don't know is what happened to these photographed documents which are missing. *You* know."

Liddel sat looking at him, despairing.

"Where are they?" Roger insisted.

Liddel said: "How could you have found out all this?"

"It came out step by step, as it always does."

"My wife?"

"Is at Scotland Yard. The more you tell us now, the less trying her ordeal will be."

Liddel said hesitantly: "I have tried to save her because I blamed myself for causing her to—become a traitor. I discovered that she was photographing secret papers; that was why I retired when I did. Nothing could be done about the past, and, once retired, there was no danger of losing further secrets, but one set of photographs never left my house. I saw her in my study with her camera, and later found the developed photographs. They dealt with NATO plans in the event of war. I destroyed them before they could be passed on. The harm was done with the others, only these really mattered. I thought that all I needed to do was to hold my peace, and perhaps help to restore hers. I knew she was giving them to Lancelot, guessed she killed him because he started to blackmail her."

"And if you'd been hanged, she would have gone unpunished."

"Her misery and the hatred she felt were punishment," Liddel said wearily. "She could do no more harm to the nation, and I was not prepared to make my own escape by bringing about her downfall. I am an old man, Mr. West, and I have served some useful purpose. Only I can measure my own success and failure, and for my failure I was prepared to go through with this. I wish that had been possible, I do not want her to suffer more. But it is inevitable now." He shivered. "Do the others know?"

"Yes. And they did everything they could to help you."

"There is always light as well as darkness," Liddel said.

"There is one ray of light two people badly need," said Roger, after a pause. He framed his words carefully. "Francesca and the man she wants to marry must have it. You haven't met the man. I think you would like him."

Liddel said : "When my mind is clearer I can think about that, not now. Francesca —"

"You must think of it now. He was orphaned, many years ago, and has lived in America most of his life."

"I don't understand you," Liddel said.

"Do you know your natural son?" Roger paused. "His name, where he lives, anything about him?"

"Surely you know him, too," said Liddel in astonishment. "You mentioned him to me. He is Louis Kane."

* * * *

There was little left to clear up. In the next few days the Harrings were caught; they would serve long sentences. M.I.5 were already after the spy ring and uncovering very big stuff. They knew that Lancelot Hay had paid most of the money he'd received to a foreign power's embassy in

London; the same power's New York embassy had paid Al Maloney senior, in dollars.

One other discovery was pieced together from Mrs. Liddel's incoherent ramblings, which placed the final piece into the jigsaw.

Mrs. Liddel had had an *affaire* with Al Maloney years before. Maloney had threatened to tell Liddel – and said he would keep quiet if she gave him a photostat of a document. From then on, terrified of her husband learning of the *affaire*, she had been forced by the older Maloney to do whatever he had wanted.

Then she had discovered about her husband's natural son.

She had allowed herself to be drawn deeply into spying because of her *affaire* before marriage, and he had been unfaithful after their marriage.

She had begun to hate Liddel.

Life had become too difficult for her, and slowly at first, almost imperceptibly, she went mad.

* * * *

Francesca and Maloney called on Roger in Bell Street, Chelsea, and Janet admitted them.

"We got round to talking about you last night, and decided it would be good to see you again before we leave. We're going home," Maloney added, and gripped Francesca's arm. "You won't be surprised at that."

"I've expected it," Roger said.

"You will stay for a cup of tea, won't you?" said Janet. She hurried out of the room, and the others sat down.

Maloney was looking his most handsome; Francesca, in a lightweight suit of gray-and-blue overcheck, was at her best. There was no sign of the strain of the past few weeks, or of the trial. Her mother had been sent to Broadmoor, after being found insane. Her father had died a few days before the trial. Kane was serving a ten years' sentence for his part in the crimes; the police accepted his statement that Smith had given him the gun, and he had not been charged with murder.

"I'll say this for you," Maloney said, "you were a better

detective than I thought at one time. Do I have to say I'm sorry?"

"You're more honest than I ever suspected," Roger murmured slyly.

Francesca laughed.

"We're off on the *Queen Elizabeth* tonight," said Maloney. "If you're interested, Tony is staying in England, he says it would seem like running away if he left right now. He's a good chap."

"We've learned that," said Roger.

"I'll tell you another thing," went on Maloney. "I met one of your men a few days ago — Burnaby. Sergeant Burnaby now, he tells me, and in the Flying Squad. He approves of you."

"Burnaby's all right," said Roger.

"Mr. West." Francesca smiled a smile that most men would give much to earn. "I think it's time we really told you why we came. It is to say thank you. To tell you that we shall always feel proud to have known you, and that we shall always remember you."